"I'VE HAD IT WITH YOU!"

Jaime Sommers screamed at Oscar Goldman.

"Jaime, listen to me—budgets are budgets!"

"You know what you can do with your budget. And don't bother to call me back until you're ready to talk about some money—and I mean big money!"

All Jaime really wanted was to find her own life again, to settle down in peaceful Ojai, California. But she was the only person on earth who might be able to stop Carlton Harris. If her bionics didn't fail her again....

Harris owned a vast conglomerate of companies, and he was shrewd. He mixed legitimate and illegitimate deals skillfully, and the OSI hadn't been able to get the goods on him, although three agents had already died trying. Now it was Jaime's turn, her first mission all on her own. All she had to do was look beautiful and convince Carlton Harris that he really didn't want to take her apart to see what made her tick. And get the goods. And get out alive.

THE BIONIC WOMAN

WELCOME HOME, JAIME
a novel by Eileen Lottman

Based on the Universal television series
THE BIONIC WOMAN
Created for television by Kenneth Johnson
Based on the novel **CYBORG** by Martin Caidin
Adapted from the episode **WELCOME HOME, JAIME**
Written by Kenneth Johnson

A BERKLEY MEDALLION BOOK
published by
BERKLEY PUBLISHING CORPORATION

Chapter One

"Mrs. Austin, I think I'll beat you today," Steve Austin boasted as he and Jaime walked onto the tennis courts.

"Wrong on two counts," she replied, laughing. "I won't be Mrs. Austin for another week. And there's no way you can beat the pro who set Billie Jean back at Forest Hills." Her long tawny hair was tied back in a bright ribbon, and her huge gray eyes sparkled with the pure joy of being alive, and in love.

Steve looked at her, a momentary flash of concern. "You're feeling okay now, huh?"

"Well enough to beat you," she replied cheerfully. But she knew what he was referring to. "I apologized to your mom this morning. She's such an angel. She said it was just pre-marriage jitters. But—it's just not like me. I don't know what was the matter with me yesterday. I feel awful about snapping at her like that."

"Probably just the anticipation of losing this match to me," Steve said lightly.

Jaime grinned. The bright morning sun warmed her and glinted off Steve's dark hair, and she thought for the millionth time how lucky they were, how handsome he was, what a very special and happy pair they made. "We'll see about that," she laughed, and ran on long slender legs to the far court.

"Service," she called. She tossed the ball high and straight, and her right arm came up to smash it down and over.

"Fault," Steve called. "Long."

Jaime Sommers felt a chill rush through her body. It was almost as if an alien force entered, jarring her into a rage over which she had no control.

"What do you mean, long? It was good!" she shouted angrily.

Steve straightened from his receiver's crouch, and shielded his eyes from the sun to peer at her across the court. "No kidding," he said, "it was out—"

"I say it was good," she declared.

Steve shook his head. "Honest, sweetheart—"

She interrupted, furious. "Steve, I'm a ranking pro and you're . . . I think I know a good serve when I see it."

Puzzled, but figuring it wasn't worth arguing about, Steve shrugged. "Okay, maybe you're right."

Her voice rose to a scream. "Don't patronize me! I don't need that!"

"Jaime, I'm not—"

Her right hand swung the racquet in a high arc, and before Steve could finish his thought, she hurled it with incredible force straight at his head. The racquet whistled with the speed of a deadly projectile, and he had to drop to the ground with all the agility his special

2

body afforded him to avoid being hit. It sailed a scant inch from his head and knifed through the back fence like an axe, cutting a hole through the steel mesh and soaring out of sight far beyond the courts.

Steve looked up at Jaime. She was standing quietly, looking bewildered. Her fury had drained out of her, and she was as stunned as he was.

"Steve? What happened?"

He picked himself up and moved toward the net. "Don't you remember?"

Her lovely eyes were soft again, confused and a bit frightened. "We were playing tennis, and—" She looked at her right hand. It was trembling, and her racquet was gone. She looked back at Steve and then behind him to the jagged hole in the fence. Tears welled up in her eyes. "Steve, what's happening to me?" she said, seriously frightened now. Her arm was quivering uncontrollably.

He leaped over the net with one easy motion and dropped his own racquet to take her in his arms. She leaned into his strength. His firm tan skin was warm, and his powerful arms were tender.

"Come on," he said gently. She clung to him as he led her off the court.

"You haven't told Rudy, have you, about the little problems you've been having?" he asked her as he drove swiftly over the roads toward the medical complex of the Bionic Research Lab.

Jaime shook her head slowly. "It didn't seem important," she said. "I know you had trouble adjusting, and, well, I thought it was just that. I kept thinking it would go away."

Her long hair was blowing free in the open-top car,

and she looked like a model of perfect health and vitality. Steve glanced at her from time to time as he drove, marveling at her beauty and trying not to let her feel his conviction that there was something very, very wrong.

A few hours later, Steve was seated in the office of Dr. Rudy Wells, waiting for the results of the emergency tests on Jaime. Oscar Goldman was there, too, of course. Oscar was the director of the OSI, the Office of Strategic Intelligence, which was an umbrella organization overseeing an enormous complex of various civilian and military intelligence agencies. Oscar was the man responsible for Steve's special life, and now Jaime's, too.

Rudy came into the office, finally. He held an X-ray slide in his hand, and, without preamble, he pinned it in the viewing box and switched on the light.

"You can see it here on the picture of her skull," he said, pointing to a smudged area on the slide.

"What is it?" Oscar asked. His face never revealed anxiety or tension. He was virtually unflappable, but as he leaned forward to peer at the X-ray, his intense energy could be felt almost palpably in the room.

"It's plasma," Rudy answered. "Jaime's body is producing massive amounts of white blood cells to fight off the foreign bodies in her system."

"You mean she has an infection?" Steve asked.

"No," Rudy answered gravely. "It's her bionics, Steve. Jaime's body is rejecting her bionics."

The world's first and only bionic man sat with his head in his hands, trying to straighten out his thoughts and his emotions. He was responsible for the fact that Jaime was here now. He had begged Oscar to save her

4

from spending the rest of her life as a hopeless cripple after the skydiving accident that smashed her legs and her whole right side. He alone knew what it meant to be a combination of natural human being and man-made computerized replacement parts. What he hadn't anticipated was that the experiment might not work twice.

Steve was nicknamed the "six million dollar man" by those few who knew about him. That's how much it had cost to put him together after the crash landing of the rocket plane he had been testing, the crash that left him a basket case until Oscar Goldman got hold of him.

Oscar had been waiting years for such an opportunity, the chance to test the new science of bionics. The word *bionic* derived from Greek roots, meaning "in a manner approximating life." Bionics was, in a sense, the highest tribute to the success of natural evolution. Bionic scientists realized that there had never been an instrument more efficient for use in grasping and manipulating than the human hand, with its fingers and apposite thumb. No temperature-regulating device had ever been invented that could be as sensitive and finely tuned as that found in higher mammals. Bionic scientists had it their work to create mechanical and electronic devices which would duplicate exactly the actions of natural body functions. And, though it sounded fanciful, it was quite logical. The fact that a human hand works is ample proof that a properly constructed artificial hand will also work. The key phrase is *properly constructed*. When it was first developed in the late 1950's, bionics concerned itself with little more than the production of artificial limbs.

But before long, the science grew to include such disciplines as biology, medicine, cybernetics, information theory, and mechanical, electrical, and nuclear engineering. By the mid-1970's, scientists at the Bionic Research Laboratory had the ability to produce a bionic man. The crash of Steve Austin's M3F5 in 1973 brought them the man. Oscar Goldman brought them the money.

There was little excuse for a pure research facility such as the BRL to spend a great deal of money on one man just to prove that it could be done. The nation's veterans' hospitals were already crowded with multiple amputees, many of whom would have eagerly accepted the chance to walk again. But Steve Austin was special. He was an Air Force colonel with a great deal of flight training. He was an astronaut who, in the final Apollo 17 mission, had spent more time on the moon's surface than any other man from earth. He had a perfect cover for a covert operation. He was not only a scientist in his own right, but also an expert on rockets and other military systems.

There was a catch, of course. Steve Austin, once repaired and made better than ever physically, would devote his life to the work of the OSI. He would be America's newest and most exotic secret weapon.

Dr. Rudy Wells kept Steve unconscious for weeks, using an electrosleep process. By thus manipulating the astronaut's brain waves, the doctor could perform extensive surgery without running the risks inherent in the use of conventional anesthetics. Steve's torn heart valve was replaced with an artificial one. The fractured part of his skull was removed and replaced by a plate made of cesium, an alkali metal light yet strong, capable of withstanding a blow ten times that which would normally crush human bones. His ribs were replaced with ribs fabricated of vitallium, joined one to the other with artificial tendons. The entire rib cage was extrajoined to the breastbone with silastic, a variant of silicone rubber. The metal ribs were embedded with fine wires, forming an excellent radio antenna.

Steve's jaw was repaired with appropriate applications of metal, ceramics, and plastic. New teeth, made of nylon, were installed. His left eye was bionic, too—based on the theory of the photomultiplier tube which incorporated a twenty-power zoom lens activated by will and light amplification by a factor of ten million.

And he had three bionic limbs—both legs and his left arm. To the arm and leg stumps Rudy Wells attached bones made of a stainless alloy. The attachment points, as well as key undamaged natural bone points throughout his body, were reinforced with alloy in order to allow the extra strength imparted by the limbs. Actual nerves and muscle were attached to bionic nerves and muscle, the natural nerve impulses amplified to bionic levels by a maze of sensors and generators. Each limb had a miniature nuclear generator creating heat which was then transformed into energy by a thermopile. Each limb had thousands of sensors duplicating the touch and temperature sensing nerves of an actual human limb. These sensors fed impulses into servomechanisms which allowed Steve to apply just as much force as was needed for a certain task. Whether the task was breaking down a concrete wall or lifting a teacup, Steve could do it naturally, without thinking about it, as one does with a natural limb. The entire setup was run by three miniaturized computers, one for each leg and the arm. Surrounding the mechanism was a sheath of alloy, sponge, and plastiskin designed to duplicate the form of Steve's natural limbs. Excess heat from the generators was used to simulate normal skin temperature. Hairs were embedded in the plastiskin, which also received a photo-chemical dye treatment allowing it to tan somewhat when exposed to the sun. When the bionic transformation was complete, all Steve was unable to do was to cut his nails.

But artificial fingertips tend to be insensitive, and a cybernetic hand could crush human bone with no more effort than was needed to pulp a rose. So they had added vibrating pads, delicate supersensors, transmitters, and feedback. Now the steel-boned hands that could kill with a single transmitted impulse could also gently caress a lover's skin.

Steve, after an initial resentment of being on call to the OSI and Oscar Goldman for the rest of his life, made his emotional adjustment. And after a while, when the bionic equipment had become natural to him and he had been on many missions all over the world, he began to like it.

Then the most important thing of all had happened to him. Steve had fallen in love. She was the girl he had grown up with, but one day they looked at each other with new eyes and they were like any two young people anywhere, convinced that what they had was unique. This time, he and Jaime were no longer children daring each other to mischief, or teenagers dreaming of the world they would conquer someday. Mature and whole, they had fallen deeply in love.

They were both natural athletes and in their courtship they rejoiced in the delights of riding, skiing, surfing, playing hard competitive games together. They had gone skydiving together, floating and tumbling weightlessly through the air with the earth far below them. And suddenly Jaime's chute had tangled and collapsed a hundred feet over a grove of trees. When she had landed, both legs and her right arm were shattered. Her right ear had been ripped from her head.

At the hospital, the doctor had told Steve, "It's amazing that she's alive at all. Her legs have so many breaks we still haven't counted them all. The hemorrhaging from her ear seems to indicate damage to the cochlea and the corti—probably a total loss of hearing. Her right arm and shoulder are torn beyond our power to mend them. I'm sorry, Colonel Austin. We'll try to save her, but there's only so much we can do. Maybe someday we'll find a way to repair bodies so badly broken."

Steve sat by Jaime's bed for hours, willing her to live, to be well again, wishing he could project some of his own overabundant strength into her crushed body. And then she had regained consciousness, barely.

"I guess...I really...messed...up," she said with great effort.

"Hey, cut out that kind of talk," he said, trying to smile. "You'll be okay."

"No...it's...over...over..." Her voice trailed off weakly.

The doctor's words came back to Steve. Someday, the doctor had said. But Steve knew someday was now. He knew what he had to do. He leaned down close to Jaime's pale face.

9

"Jaime," he whispered, "there may be a way. Will you let me try? Will you trust me? Jaime?"

After what seemed to him like a desperately futile wait, Jaime's eyelids fluttered, and she mustered enough strength to nod, just once, before slipping into unconsciousness again. Steve rose from her bedside and picked up the telephone.

Within the hour, Oscar Goldman was at the hospital. He and Steve had a heated discussion in the little waiting area down the hall from Jaime's room.

"No, Steve. It's just not possible," Oscar said flatly.

"You know that's not true," Steve said, his blue eyes flashing. "I'm the living proof that it is possible."

"I don't mean the technology. Of course we might be able to repair her body, to put her back together . . . that might be possible. But there are too many other considerations." Oscar was a wiry six-footer, whose deceptively mild manner was a thin cover for his incredible talents. He was a genius at sizing people up, and a man with an extraordinary grasp of science and its limitless possibilities. His specialty was weapons technology, but he had the rare ability to correlate an enormous range of facts from various disciplines. His authority was as high as anyone in government service, and Steve knew the decision to save Jaime's life was entirely in Oscar's hands.

"I asked you here to help, Oscar, and so far all I've gotten is a handful of red tape."

Oscar looked uncomfortable. He was the man who called the shots and yet—on this particular team—Steve was his only player. Oscar had run into Steve's independent attitude before. He couldn't afford to lose his cooperation.

"There's a woman in there, Oscar, who has been left with two ruined and useless legs, an arm and shoulder crushed beyond repair, and no hearing in one ear—and you have the power to put her back together, better than new, just like you did me," Steve went on.

"Steve, bionic limbs cost millions, and it would mean bringing Rudy and the bionics team in here. How can I justify the expenditure?"

"How did you justify me?"

"That was different. There was a need—"

"There still is." Steve cut him short. "They're always looking for a new angle, a new way to test their theories. Oscar, think of what an asset Jaime could be to you. Her cover as a tennis pro is even better than mine. There are a lot of places she could get into that I might not be able to..."

"Steve—"

"And she's got the head for it, too. She's bright, clever, well adjusted..."

"Steve, you're in love with her."

"What's that got to do with it?"

"Everything. Because right now you'd sell your soul to save her, in fact you'd be willing to commit her and yourself to anything. But later on, if we needed to use Jaime, to send her out on missions, you'd change your mind. You know how dangerous—"

"I won't change my mind, Oscar. I swear it."

There was a long pause. Oscar looked at Steve, and Steve returned his penetrating stare with a steady, serious plea.

"What about Jaime?" Oscar asked finally. "What

does she have to say about working with us the rest of her life—''

''She's dying, Oscar,'' Steve interrupted passionately. ''You're the only one who can help. *Will* you help?''

They looked at each other, two friends who had been through so much together.

''Please,'' Steve said simply.

Oscar was startled to see tears in the clear blue eyes. He reached out to touch Steve's broad shoulder in a gesture that said it all.

Chapter Two

Jaime's recovery had been relatively quick, and apparently complete. At first, she was appalled to discover that her right arm and both legs were "artificial." She even had a moment when she believed she would have been better left to die.

"What did you let them do to me, Steve?" she cried out when she first looked at her arm. It was perfectly healed, without scars, but she couldn't move it. Steve had told her, hesitantly at first and then with a rush of words, that it was a bionic arm, and that she would learn to use it perfectly and find it even better than the one she had lost.

"Believe me, I know how you feel," he had concluded, sympathetic to her dismay.

"How could you know how I feel? I don't want to be a freak!" she wept.

"Jaime—"

"I just want to die! Don't you understand? Let me die!"

Steve became angry. "Jaime, don't tell me about

wanting to die! Look at me!''

She turned her tear-stained face to him. He picked up a heavy metal chair from her bedside and bent it completely out of shape with his left hand. Jaime watched in stunned silence.

"I know exactly how tough it is. I went through exactly what you're going through," he said.

"You...your arm is...bionic...like mine?"

He nodded. "Both legs, too. And an eye."

"An eye?" She was fascinated now, her tears forgotten. "Which one?" she asked, peering closely.

"You tell me," he said. He bent down to her. Their eyes were inches apart. She stared breathlessly at the familiar blueness, the soft lashes, and the loving look she knew so well.

"I...I can't tell," she whispered.

Steve straightened up. "I'll be here to help you, Jaime. But it's a lot of hard work and sometimes it gets depressing, believe me. But you've got to try, Jaime, you've got to! Okay?"

She nodded slowly, never taking her eyes from his. "But..."

"But what?"

"Well, it's just that you'll never be able to look at me again, maybe like—to admire my legs or something—knowing so much of me isn't really me."

Steve looked at her solemnly, and nodded. "Yeah," he said. "I guess you'll feel the same way every time you look at me."

Jaime was outraged. "What are you talking about?" she said. "I love you. It doesn't make any difference whether you're bionic or—" She stopped, realizing that he had played a loving trick on her. She smiled and reached up to hug him.

After a long moment, she sighed. "Steve..."

"Hmmmm?"

"Will I be able to play the violin when my hand is better—when I learn how to control it?"

"Well, sure."

"That's really wonderful," she said, grinning. "I couldn't play it before."

Steve winced. "No doubt about it, you're getting well."

Jaime's recuperation was a wonderful time for both of them. Steve stayed by her side as much as he could, encouraging her and working with her to learn total control over the delicate mechanisms which were part of her body now. Together they jogged—at speeds up to thirty-five miles an hour—and swam and rode and played tennis again.

And then came the inevitable day when Oscar called in his marker. He needed Jaime for a special mission, and she was ready. Steve protested, but reminded of his promise and faced with Jaime's eagerness to repay the debt of her very life and happiness, he had to give in. They had worked the mission together, and it had turned out all right, despite a sudden flareup—a momentary loss of control—in Jaime's bionic right hand.

But it had only been a matter of more time to gather her strength, they all agreed. The mission against Carlton Harris had turned out okay after all, and after a few more weeks of therapy and tests, even Steve finally agreed that Jaime seemed to be in perfect shape. They set a date for their wedding.

Then it started to snowball. The little minor tremors

in Jaime's right hand flared up unexpectedly, and there was an occasional spasm which caused her to crush a wineglass when she only meant to clink it against Steve's in a lighthearted toast. There was the flare of uncharacteristic temperament, raising her voice at Steve's mother whom she had loved since childhood...then the incident on the tennis court, the racquet flung bionically through the back fence. And now, Steve sat with Rudy and Oscar staring at an X-ray which showed that Jaime's body was rejecting the bionic implants.

"But it didn't happen to me," Steve protested.

"And it doesn't happen to all heart transplant patients, either," Rudy explained. "But to some, it does." He studied the X-ray. "Since the prime area of bionic control is centered in this portion of the brain, the plasma is building up there in intense concentration," he said. "It's apparently creating intermittent pressure on this block of nerves. It can have very serious neurological implications. It could bring excruciating pain...."

"Even alter her personality?" Steve asked thoughtfully.

"Yes," Rudy said. "Just as drastically as you described. Maybe even worse."

"Can it be arrested?" Oscar asked.

"I don't know," Rudy answered slowly, "but some of the blood vessels are already rupturing under the pressure. She's in a lot of danger. We've got to operate immediately."

"Let's go, then," Oscar said. Rudy snapped off the X-ray light, and strode from the room without another word.

16

A few minutes later, Steve and Oscar joined him in the operating room, dressed in surgical robes and masks. They stood in the back of the white room, hardly daring to breathe.

"How're the vital signs?" They heard Rudy's tense tone through his mask.

"Low."

"Specifics."

"Pulse thready...about fifteen. Systolic is about seventy over...over...I can't get a diastolic at all."

"She's shocky," reported another nurse in an urgent voice.

"I'd better go in. Give me the laser drill...calibrate four millimeters...Bruno, give me a better picture on the videcon X-ray monitor."

All eyes turned briefly to the flashing red light that indicated the rate of Jaime's heartbeat.

"Doctor...I'm losing her."

Steve moved forward involuntarily. Oscar checked him with a firm grip on his arm. He stepped back, feeling more helpless than he ever had in his life.

"Give her two cc's adrenalin, intracardial. Drop the line voltage on the electroanesthetic...Where's the damned X-ray monitor?"

"Here, Dr. Wells."

"She's still slipping," the control doctor reported.

Steve felt his forehead bristle with perspiration. He held his breath to hear Rudy Wells's next words.

"Oh, dear God," the surgeon murmured. "She's got a massive cerebral hemorrhage."

"The vital signs are going, doctor."

Oscar couldn't hold Steve back now. As if sleepwalking, the six million dollar man moved closer to the operating table.

"Jaime . . ."

Rudy's voice broke. "She can't hear you, Steve," he said sadly.

Steve leaned down to his love's still lips. He pressed close to her right ear, the one that would surely hear him if any life remained.

"Jaime . . . I love you . . . I've always loved you . . ."

He laid his hand on hers. Her fingers twitched almost imperceptibly, and then tugged at his in a last gesture of love. And farewell.

Jaime was medically dead.

Steve turned blindly from her. Oscar took his arm and guided him from the operating room in silence.

But there was one man in the room who refused to believe in the evidence of all the scientific technology before their eyes. As Rudy Wells stepped back from the table, his young assistant moved a step closer to the lifeless patient.

"Rudy, let me try," Michael Marchetti said simply.

The older doctor's eyes lifted in a quizzical expression over the mask that covered the rest of his face. "Your cryogenics?" he said, remembering the research that Michael was devoted to.

The young doctor nodded. "The heart has stopped, but the brain keeps functioning for a while. Let me try, Rudy, before that function stops, too. Please."

Rudy Wells looked down at the dead patient shrouded in surgical sheets. He nodded once, and the nurses caught his signal. Rudy stepped back to allow Michael to take over. He called for his special equipment, and within seconds the machines were wheeled in and he began making the vital connections to Jaime's heart and brain.

It seemed like hours. Over and over again, Michael pumped and measured, shocked and massaged, froze and thawed.

The temperature in the operating room was lowered so radically that fingers were bitten to keep the feeling in them. The heart-lung machine was attached to Jaime to keep her blood oxygenated, to try to ward off brain damage.

Rudy and his backup team worked to relieve the hemorrhage while Michael administered his cryogenic therapy. The cooling agent retarded her body's metabolism and powerful antitoxins were combined to ward off cellular damage.

Michael pressed the electrodes of the cardiac shock device against Jaime's motionless chest. The nurse hit the switch and the current caused her body to arch once, twice, and then—the steady tone of the oscillo-scope blipped!

Again. Again. The irregular pulsations started to come with increasing frequency. The limp respirator sack began to tremble slightly, and then it filled with a breath of air. Jaime was breathing!

"By God, you did it!" Rudy gasped. They had all been holding their breaths, and now exhalations of relief and wonder rose in vapor clouds all through the freezing O.R.

"It's a miracle," a nurse said, not even knowing that she said it.

"We seem to specialize in miracles around here," Michael said. He was a shy young man, embarrassed by the admiring glances he was getting.

19

"Nice work" Rudy said as they were dressing down in the scrub room later.

"I learned it all from you," Michael said.

"Not that part!" Rudy grinned across the low sink. "Well, we've got to keep her under very close watch for quite a while now. The probability of brain damage is high."

"She wasn't really gone that long," Michael said, letting hope transcend his judgment for once.

"We'll have to wait and see," was all Rudy would say.

Jaime's recovery was slow and perilous. She was in a coma for a very long time. Five separate times, they thought she was slipping away again. Steve was not allowed to see her—in fact, Oscar sent him on a mission halfway around the world, not even telling him that Jaime had been revived, for fear that he would have to go through the anguish of losing her again.

At last, her condition began to stabilize. Her body was no longer rejecting the bionics, and they began to schedule tests which would determine whether or not she had suffered any kind of permanent damage. She seemed to be her even-tempered, good-natured self again, despite the weakness of body which made them put off testing her mental and emotional faculties for a while.

Jaime had only been fully conscious for two days when Steve demanded to see her. His arms filled with fresh yellow daisies, he opened the door to her room. His heart bounded against his rib cage when he saw her wide eyes smiling at him from the bed where she lay.

"Hello," she said. "Who are you?"

Chapter Three

"No, only what they've been telling me lately," she said calmly. "I know that I died, and that Michael brought me back—the nurses told me that, although I think maybe they weren't supposed to. But, Oscar, it's as though I never existed before I came back to life in this hospital. It's so strange."

"Yes, of course it is," Oscar said. "But it's not the worst thing that might have happened, is it? We can reprogram your memory, and Rudy is reasonably certain that the part of your brain which suffered the . . . illness . . . can be slowly brought back, too. Just be patient, Jaime, and be certain that everything in the world which can be done is being done for you."

"Oscar, did Rudy tell you about my nightmares?"

"Yes."

"About the pain that goes with them? I have these flashes of—I guess they must be memories, I don't know. Scenes, like images crossing my mind without warning, and with them comes the awful pain. Excruciating, unbearable pain, Oscar, it frightens me, and then I get to thinking maybe it's better not to remember at all. Not if remembering means so much pain.''

"They're testing you for areas which don't cause the pain, Jaime, and believe me, nobody wants you to suffer. Your brain can be reminded only of the pleasant things—''

"But they are pleasant, some of them! I want to look back, because I think there's somebody there ... somebody I loved. And I was happy, I think. But I can't stand the pain.''

"Jaime—''

"Oh, I know, Oscar. I don't mean to complain. You must think I'm a terrible ingrate, complaining instead of being grateful just to be alive!''

"Nobody thinks that,'' he said.

"Well, the re-education program is very interesting,'' she said in an attempt to be cheerful again. "I know my name, and how I got these incredible legs and this arm and this ear—thank you for that, Oscar—and I know, oh, lots of things. Everything they've told me in the past few weeks.''

"Well, you stick to all that and don't worry about the things that went before.''

"Easier said than done. But I'm trying, Oscar. Really I am.''

"Right,'' he said. He stood up to leave. "Uh—do you want to see Steve again? I believe he's waiting right out there.''

"Steve? Oh, isn't that nice? No, I don't think so, right now. I'm kind of sleepy. Will you explain to him? He really doesn't have to be so nice. I know we grew up together, but he's really not my brother or anything.''

Oscar hesitated a moment and then smiled a little sadly. "I'll tell him," he said, and left the room. Jaime's eyes closed and she fell into a light, troubled, pain-filled sleep.

They were able to reprogram Jaime's brain with all the necessary information within a few months, and her body healed with satisfactory speed. She and Steve Austin became friends, and as the only two bionic people in the world (or at least as far as the government of the United States could determine), they worked together again on missions for Oscar and the OSI.

All seemed normal, even buoyantly enthusiastic, except for the occasional bouts of intense pain which still assailed Jaime once in a while. The love which had been so deep and so solid between them existed now only in Steve's memory. Any attempt to remind Jaime of that part of her past seemed to being on those terrifying attacks again. And so the decision was made to cease all efforts to remind Jaime of the way things used to be. She lived only in the present, and she was generally making a good adjustment to that.

"Will she always be like that?" Steve demanded, finally.

Rudy Wells shook his head. "It might be possible to restore her memory surgically," he said.

"Might be?"

"She will have to go back under strict observation, and when we know exactly what is causing the pain associated with the memory, Michael and I think we can separate those elements. Maybe.''

"It's me," Steve said slowly. "It's memories that involve me which she can't tolerate. I'm not good for

Jaime.''

Oscar Goldman narrowed his eyes behind the black-rimmed glasses. ''What do you suggest, Steve?''

''Send her to Rudy's other complex in Colorado Springs,'' Steve said slowly. ''Away from here. Away from me.''

''For how long?''

Steve looked out of the window. With his bionic eye, he focused on a sun-dappled path under the trees several hundred yards away. Jaime was walking with Michael, and they were laughing. She was holding his hand.

''For as long as it takes,'' Steve said sadly.

A few days later, he said goodbye to her in the parking lot outside the medical complex. Michael was at the wheel of the car.

Jaime looked up at Steve. ''I don't know what it is,'' she said, ''but sometimes I look at you, and I feel that there was something more. Was there?'' She gazed searchingly at him with the candid, open question. If he tried to remind her...no, he must not.

''I'm your friend, Jaime. I always was and I always will be,'' was all he said.

She leaned up to kiss him.

''Bye.''

''Bye.''

She waved as Michael turned the car out of the driveway, and Steve waved back until she was out of sight.

Jaime gloried in the clear air and magnificent mountain scenery of Colorado. She was a willing subject for all the tests Michael and Rudy could devise, submitting to the pain as it came in waves, knowing it was necessary to do so, frequently falling into unconsciousness from the intolerable stress, but awakening with renewed determination to get on with it.

Finally, they were ready for the operation.

"It may or may not restore your memory, Jaime," Rudy explained to her carefully. "But we do think that we can relieve the pain, at the very least."

"I understand," she answered. "Let's do it, please."

"Bad, huh?" Michael murmured. They had grown very close over the past months.

"You know it!"

She came out of the anesthetic like a cloud wafting across an early-morning landscape. Dreamily, the mist cleared and she could almost hear the voices that murmured outside her door. I have a bionic ear, she remembered. But her head was feeling too floaty just then to turn toward the sounds. She lay quietly, waiting for the cloud to drift into the clearing that she knew must lie just beyond the grogginess.

"She's doing well."

"Yes."

"What percentage of her damaged brain cells do you figure we've regenerated?"

"All of them we're going to."

"And restored at least a part of her memory?"

"As far as we can determine without her conscious help."

"Mixed blessings, Michael? If she remembers Steve and their life together, what they were and were going to be to each other, you'll probably lose her."

"Yes, but at least maybe she'll lose the pain."

The two doctors were startled by the little light that suddenly flashed on above Jaime's door. They entered at once.

Her eyes were open and she was smiling weakly. Her hand was on the call button.

"Hi, there," Michael said. He sat on the edge of her bed and took her wrist in his, counting the pulse beats as they talked.

"Hi," she answered faintly. "How'm I doing?"

"You're going to have to tell us. What's your name?"

"Jaime Sommers." She managed a little lopsided grin at him.

"Do you know us?"

She looked from Michael's nice face up to the older doctor's. "You're Rudy...and this is Michael, of course. But I knew that before."

"Right. Feel strong enough to try going back a little further?" Michael asked. She nodded. "Okay. Where did you go to school?"

"Carnegie Tech," she answered promptly. The reaction on his face told her that this was part of the landscape she had not recognized before. An enormous freshet of relief, combined with a lively curiosity, washed over her. "Yeah...I do remember..." she said.

"What did you major in?" Michael continued.

"Education." Her voice was thin, but her excitement and delight came through loud and clear for all of them. "I was going to be a teacher," she said. Tears welled in her eyes. "Oh, Michael...I remember. I remember!" She pushed herself up off the pillow, both arms reaching out to embrace him in her gratitude. She held him tightly.

Michael Marchetti's own emotions were barely under control. His professional bedside manner was being sorely tested. Jaime Sommers was an extraordinarily beautiful young woman. In the recent months since he had literally brought her back from the dead, they had become more than professional doctor and patient, sharing long walks and talks together as well as medical therapy and care.

She's engaged to marry Steve Austin, he reminded himself sternly, holding her in his arms. Even if she doesn't know it herself. Or does she . . . ?

"Easy, now," he said with an effort even the sharp-eyed Rudy Wells couldn't guess at. "Let's try another area. Do you remember Steve?"

The hospital room was silent while Jaime eased back onto her pillow, searching the mists for another break in the view. "Steve . . ." she repeated thoughtfully, looking at Michael.

A clearing in the clouds, and Jaime caught a mental glimpse of a broad-shouldered young man running in the rain. "Sure," she said now. "My bionic friend."

"What do you remember about him?" Michael asked. If he anticipated her answer with a heavy heart, there was no sign of it.

Jaime reflected on the memories brought back to her by the mame of Steve Austin. "Well . . . he's bionic. And he's cute, and he worries about me a lot."

She saw Michael look up to exchange a glance with Rudy. Then he looked back at her. What a nice man Michael was, so gentle and patient. She wondered what it was he was expecting her to recall.

"Do you remember anything else about Steve?" he

asked.

She remembered a little tousle-haired boy on a swing, and then a lanky teenager who talked about becoming an astronaut. "We grew up together?" she ventured. "At least, I think we did."

Dr. Wells spoke for the first time. "Yes," he reassured her. "Now, Jaime, do you remember anything about your skydiving accident?"

"What?" she exclaimed. "I've never been skydiving. Have I?" she finished weakly, seeing the look that passed between the two doctors.

Michael patted her hand. Rudy covered his concern with a broad smile. "You're still groggy from the operation," he said, "and we've tired you more than we should have. We're going to have to do a lot more testing, naturally. You rest now, all right?"

Jaime nodded wearily. Her elation had drained away with the realization that she still had a long way to go before she was fully recovered. Michael got up from the bed, and before the two men had left the room, their troubled patient closed her eyes. She dreamed not of the past, but of an uncertain future. But there was no pain.

Steve was waiting in Rudy's office. He jumped to his feet when the doctor entered.

"How is she?"

"Fine. She's doing remarkably well," Rudy said, sitting down behind the large desk piled high with reports and medical studies. It was not a typical medical doctor's assortment of research materials. If one looked closely at the titles, one would see a curious mix of top secret materials dealing not only with life sciences, but cybernetics, computer technology,

28

miniaturization, electronics, and weaponry technology.

"Is her memory restored?" Steve asked anxiously.

"In part, yes. It's really too early to tell, Steve, how successful this operation has been. But, yes, she remembers things she was blocked on before. School, and her friendship with you. We haven't had time to test for more than that."

"Friendship?"

Rudy smiled wryly. "Is that all you heard of what I said?" he asked.

"She doesn't remember that we were—engaged?"

"Give it time, Steve, okay?"

Steve understood about time. He had been patient before; now that it was Jaime, he would be more than patient again. For as long as it takes, he had told Oscar.

"How long will it be before you know for sure?" he asked in a calmer voice.

"No way of guessing, Steve. You understand better than anyone that this is all experimental—first time out. Let's take it one step at a time."

"Sorry, Rudy. I guess Oscar's the one I should be taking out my frustrations on. He's used to it, at any rate."

"Sure, why don't you go holler at Oscar? If he didn't thrive on it, he wouldn't stay on as head of the OSI. Nobody else could do the job, or would want to. We're just sawbones here."

"I like your modesty, Rudy. By the way, when's the world going to know about the stuff you guys are pulling off here?"

"When they're ready, Steve. When they're ready,"

Rudy said. His head was already bent over the thick file on Jaime Sommers, as he began to pore once more through the detailed study of what had gone right and what had gone wrong with the second bionic creature. Steve left the room without disturbing Rudy's concentration.

A few weeks later, Jaime was seated in one of the testing labs down the hall. She was fully dressed and looking as radiantly healthy as an ad for sunshine. Michael was drawing the blinds and allowed himself a split second of regret that dimming the light meant cutting himself off from admiring her translucent skin and the curve of her cheekbone. Stop it, he told himself silently. She belongs to someone else, and it's my job to get her to remember that.

In a moment, Rudy had started the projector, and the first slide was flashed onto the screen before Jaime. She said instantly, "New York."

"Good," Rudy commented, leaving the skyline panorama on the screen for a moment. "Now, some of these pictures are faces and places that you don't know. Others, you may recognize. And let us know immediately if you feel any pain at all."

"Don't worry," Jaime answered. She still remembered the severe spasms that had gone before this most recent operation, and she knew that if it recurred there would be no way to suffer the pain in silence.

"Okay," Rudy said, "now watch the screen."

"London," Jaime called out as Parliament loomed up in black and white. "There's Big Ben, and Westminster..."

Rudy punched up another slide. It was a tennis court. To him and Michael, it looked like any tennis court anywhere in the world, but Jaime recognized it immediately. "Wimbledon!" she said.

But the slide brought another image to Jaime's memory, one which quickly came and left before the next projected image. She saw herself on a tennis court, and she was throwing her racquet in a totally uncharacteristic rage. That was when my bionics were going out of whack, she thought. Who had she been playing with?

The next slide was up, the face of a man she had never seen before, to her knowledge. "Don't know him," she said.

Jaime grinned in the darkness when the next picture appeared. That stern countenance, tanned and taut, gentle eyes hidden behind the businesslike glasses. "That's Oscar, of course," she said.

Another cityscape. "Pittsburgh."

A college campus. "That's Carnegie Tech, where I studied teaching," Jaime announced. Then a photo of a woman. "I don't know her." A man. "Charles Moore. He taught my adolescent psych class in, uh, my sophomore year."

A sunny street appeared on the screen, its focal point a whitewashed adobe arcade shadowing a line of little shop fronts. "Oh, that looks familiar," Jaime said. "Is it Ojai?" She had grown up in that lovely California town.

Rudy didn't answer, nor did Michael. Rudy flashed another slide onto the screen, while Michael never took his eyes, accustomed now to the dark, from his close scrutiny of Jaime's reactions. The next picture was a posed portrait of an attractive couple, whose clothes and hairstyles clearly indicated that the picture had been taken somew ten or fifteen years before. Jaime took a few minutes before she said anything. "Are those my parents?"

"Yes," Rudy answered. "Do you remember them?"

Jaime had to strain to reach the memory. "They died...in an auto accident. I was sixteen," she said.

Michael spoke quickly, not troubling to hide his concern. "Yes," he said. "Do you feel like going on?"

Jaime nodded affirmatively. Her momentary sadness was a normal reaction, and she was eager to continue. It was kind of fun, remembering. "Yes, please," she said.

She commented as the slides continued. "Don't know him...that's Los Angeles...oh, there's Steve's mom and dad, Helen and Jim." Her voice became warm now. "I remember them very well. They became my legal guardians after my parents died. Go on, Rudy...don't know that place—is it Chicago?...oh, there's Forest Hills...that's Steve—wait!"'

Michael and Rudy watched her as she struggled with an elusive image. "I remember running...in the rain. Steve found me. I remember how it *hurt*—"

"Does it hurt now?"

"No, not now," she said slowly.

"You're sure?"

"Yes. It doesn't hurt now. But I remember something about Steve running after me, and I was running from the pain—was it a nightmare or did it really happen? I don't feel it now, but I remember how it felt."

"Good." Rudy's comment was more diagnostic than sympathetic, but she knew he meant it kindly. She blinked when he switched on the overhead light.

"Can't we do some more?" she asked.

"Not now," Rudy said.

"We've got to do some tests on your bionics, anyway," Michael said. He held out his hand to help her from the chair. She didn't need it, but she took it. Then she turned back to Rudy, who was already filing the slides away.

"But I'd really like to keep working on my memory," she said.

Rudy looked at her. "Jaime," he said, "we want to move much more slowly and carefully this time."

"We don't want to rush it," Michael added. "We don't want to overload you again."

Jaime understood, with a bit of a shock. After all, they had saved her life with their replacement of her own shattered nerves and muscles, cells and tissue, bones and skin. And whatever had gone wrong had been their failure, too. "You guys are still afraid I might blow a fuse again, aren't you?"

Michael's dark eyes told her all she needed to know. It was a sobering thought.

"Okay," she said lightly, hiding the cold fear she felt. "I can take a hint."

She smiled at them both, and started obediently toward the door. Passing the projector, she impulsively switched the ON button. There was the full-face portrait of big Steve Austin, now hardly visible in the light that fell across the screen. She stared at it for a moment.

Something was just beyond the edges of her mind,

33

something about Steve, her good friend, her companion in the uncharted wonders of being bionic, her old buddy she had grown up with. What was it about him that she was not remembering?

Jaime glanced quickly over at Michael, but there was nothing in his face except professional concern. She grinned to reassure him that she was fine, and with one last curious glance at the face on the screen, she left the lab.

Chapter Four

The next few weeks were joyous for Jaime. Her recuperative powers once again proved to be superb. To the closest scrutiny, Jaime Sommers was a healthy normal young woman — more attractive than most, more delighted with being alive. To Dr. Rudy Wells and to Oscar Goldman, who visited the medical complex often, she was a most gratifying example of creative scientific progress.

Dr. Michael Marchetti kept his thoughts to himself, except for his obvious pleasure in charting the constant upward graph of her test results. Since she she still did not remember the true nature of her relationship with Steve Austin, and since that memory had seemed to be the cause of her pain before, Steve stayed away from the place, checking on her progress only through Oscar.

One crisp clear afternoon, Jaime was exercising, running as swift as a panther through the green Colorado hillside inside the complex, when a stray memory reeled through her thoughts. She and Steve, inside some kind of factory, fleeing together from attackers. The name "Carlton Harris" popped into her head, but before she could sort out the experience, another voice reached her. Jaime's bionic ear picked up a normal tone of voice calling her name from nearly a mile away.

"Jaime," Michael was saying to the horizon where she had vanished, "come on in."

Knowing he was clocking her with his ever-present stopwatch and charts in hand, Jaime broke into a graceful run in the direction of his voice. She vaulted a split-rail fence as though it were a twig in her path and reached the young doctor's side in less than a minute. Exuberant, happy, grateful, she hugged him with her normal arm acting as a check on the superhuman strength of her bionic arm, which could crush him if she weren't careful.

Michael returned her hug and held her a beat longer than the moment called for. He started to kiss her, but Jaime leaned away from him ruefully. They started back to the lab.

"Michael, I do care about you, you know. And not just because you saved my life. But...I can feel that there's still so much of me I'm not in touch with yet. I...I just can't make any commitments to you — or to anyone — until I finally get it all together. Until I'm really sure who I am."

"I understand," Michael said. "Of course I do."

"Oh, Michael! It's so wonderful — so many things keep coming back to me. My childhood, my parents..."

"And no pain?" Michael asked, all pro again.

"Not so far."

"I'm glad," he said warmly.

"For all the things I do remember now, I can still feel that there's a lot I don't," Jaime said thoughtfully as they reached the lab door.

"It takes time," he assured her. He held open the door for her and they joined Rudy in the little room where he was waiting for them.

Rudy was holding a thick file. He began questioning her in a familiar routine as soon as she and Michael were seated. He asked about her fourth-grade teacher, about books she'd read as a teenager, about places she'd been in her twenty-seven years before the accident. The questions jumped around in time sequence, but a clear diagnosis of her mnemonic powers was becoming increasingly apparent to the two doctors.

"Who did you beat at Forest Hills?"

"Uh...Chris Evert...no, uh, it was Billie Jean King. Yes, it was definitely Billie Jean."

"Right," Rudy said. "How about this — describe the plane that you jumped from when you had your skydiving accident."

Jaime looked perfectly blank. Michael and Rudy watched her closely.

"I...I'm sorry. There's just nothing."

Rudy closed the file. He nodded at Michael, who began to explain carefully.

"It's pretty clear, Jaime. Your memory decreases as we get closer to the accident that almost took your life."

"Almost?" Jaime managed a grin. "I know what happened, Michael. It did take my life, and you got it back for me."

"And then just sporadic flashes of memory after the

accident," Rudy went on. "Between the first operation, the one that made you bionic, and the latest one, which seems to have restored nearly all your faculties, your memory may grow stronger — or it may never come back. Does that upset you?"

"Well," Jaime said after a thoughtful pause, "partial memory is a lot better than none at all. And at least I don't have that pain anymore. I remember that!"

"Jaime," Rudy said, "I want you to understand something. Although you have no pain with your memory now, Michael's neurological techniques are still experimental. We don't know for sure what might happen further down the line."

"You mean — my body might reject the bionics again?"

"That doesn't appear to be a problem, for now," Michael said.

"For now? Sounds like you two are telling me that I'd better live pretty much in the present," Jaime said. Her jawline tightened, but her smile did not waver as she looked from Michael to Rudy.

"That's about it," Rudy said.

The little room was heavy with unspoken emotions. But Jaime stood up, tall and straight, and they saw with enormous relief that her smile was not forced at all. "Well, then," she said, "I'll just have to take the life and limbs you two gave me and live one day at a time. And be thankful for it. Thankful to both of you."

"You're quite a woman," Michael burst out.

Jaime, avoiding his eyes, looked down at the heavy file that lay closed now on Rudy's desk. "Is that all about me?" she asked. "Can I see it now?"

"Well, since we've apparently broken the pain barrier,'' Rudy said, ''at least for the time being, I guess you're entitled to find out more about who Jaime Sommers was.''

''Is,'' she corrected him.

She took the dossier from and leaned over the desk to kiss his cheek. She turned to kiss Michael, too, and left the laboratory with a cheerful grin and a wave.

''Rudy, was everything in that file?'' Michael asked. ''Everything?''

''No. I kept out the announcement of her engagement to Steve. I'm not sure of the best way to tell her about that.''

''Uh-huh,'' Michael agreed thoughtfully.

Jaime took the file out into the grassy slope, and sat in the shade of a tree to read about her life. She turned the pages slowly, stopping for long moments to remember, or to try to remember. Some photographs and handwritten notes brought back long sequences of memory, and some brought no recollection at all. After a long while, she closed the file with a sigh and sat alone in the fading afternoon, watching the spectacular mountain sunset and allowing herself an occasional, solitary sigh.

The first time Jaime ventured onto the tennis courts behind the lab, a few days later, she discovered that her old form and style came back to her easily. The automated ball server couldn't throw anything she couldn't return with ease. The problem was in corralling the bionic strength in her right arm — instead of hitting with full or even partial power, she had to hold back, a technique not easy to learn after years of developing a professional backswing and follow-through. But she was getting her serve down perfectly, when a man's voice interrupted her concentration.

"So that's how the pros do it, huh?"

"Oscar! I didn't see you." She ran to him and hugged him.

"Well, you know how sneaky I am," Oscar said lightly. "They tell me you've read the file on yourself?"

"Yes. A lot of it I remember now, but it's still kind of hazy."

Oscar put his hand on her shoulder in an affectionate gesture. She smiled, knowing his reputation as a cold-hearted martinet. In his business, he often had to give orders which might result in someone's death, and he couldn't afford to care about the people who worked for him. But underneath, she suspected he was a pussycat. Well, since she didn't work for him, she didn't have to worry. Oscar had arranged for her to be made bionic — for her life to be saved — for two reasons, maybe three. One was pure scientific experiment — they'd never had a chance to create a bionic woman, Steve Austin being the only such creature on earth so far. The second reason was that Steve had asked them to save her life — she knew that from her file, and the relationship between Oscar and his OSI and Steve was a mutually dependent one. The third reason, if there was a third reason, Jaime was convinced, was because Oscar liked her. She liked him, too, despite his reputation as an old toughie.

"The past will probably always be a little bit mysterious to you," Oscar was saying now, "but what about the present? What would you like to do now? Go back on the tennis circuit?"

Jaime laughed. "No. That wouldn't be exactly fair.

I mean, even Jimmy Connors couldn't return a serve like this..."

She tossed the ball up and came down on it with a smashing serve that tore a smouldering hole in the Har-Tru surface of the near cross-court, then bounded through the back fence, ripping through the reinforced steel mesh as though it were a paper chain.

Oscar laughed with her, and then was quickly serious again. How many people had ever seen Oscar laugh, she wondered idly.

"I guess you're right about that," he said. "Well, what are you going to do, then?"

"I've been doing a lot of thinking about it," she answered. "You know, before I became a tennis pro, I got a degree in education. I'd always planned to be a teacher. Do you know what I'd really like, Oscar?"

"What's that?"

"To go home to Ojai. To put down some roots, or find some of the old ones again, and try teaching."

"Sounds wonderful," Oscar said.

"Yes, for me. But what about for you?"

"Me?" He seemed genuinely taken aback.

"Sure," she said, smiling. "I've got to think about what you need. You've got a big investment in your bionic woman. I probably cost as much as Steve did."

"Not quite six million," Oscar assured her seriously. "Your parts were smaller."

Jaime laughed. "All right, but you know what I mean. I owe you my life, Oscar. I can never forget that. Whenever the OSI has something that needs doing, I intend to help out. Okay?"

Oscar was thoughtful. Clearly, her offer came to him as a surprise. "Listen, Jaime — after all that you've been through, you deserve to live your own life."

"I did help you, in between my operations, didn't I? I remember some of it, in flashes. Steve and I were in a factory, or a warehouse of some kind, I remember. We were running, and that's when the pain hit me. I think I messed it up for you, Oscar. Didn't I?"

"You don't owe me anything, Jaime."

"Why, Oscar, that doesn't sound like you. I also remember Steve telling me he hated the idea that he owed you his life, at first. But you didn't have any hesitation about signing him on to work for the OSI, did you?"

"You remember too much, maybe."

Jaime laughed again, and took his hand. "I won't mess up again, Oscar. They tell me I'm in perfect shape now — physically, emotionally, all ways. No pain, and the strength of two bionic legs and an arm and an ear that can tap in on a conversation a mile away. I want to work for you if I can, Oscar."

"No, Jaime. I appreciate it, but . . . no, I can't let you do it."

She poked his chest with a gentle, jeering finger. "I can't believe it!" she laughed. "Is this really Oscar Goldman talking? I thought you were supposed to be Mister Tough Bureaucrat, huh? Now give yourself a break, will you? I'm a volunteer — you don't get many of those, I'll bet!"

Oscar couldn't help responding to her buoyant good humor. He grinned. "All right, all right. You just get yourself settled in Ojai and then we'll see about it."

Jaime threw her arms around his neck. "I mean it, Oscar. I'd better get an assignment from you soon — or I'll come and kick your door down."

"And you're just the girl who can do it," he sighed in mock terror.

"You know it!" Jaime laughed.

"Rudy says you're ready to leave here any time."

"Yes. Today, as a matter of fact," she said.

"Shall I get you a flight into Ojai?"

Jaime stooped to pick up the practice balls, and Oscar helped her as they talked. "I ve already called my own private pilot," she said. "He's on his way here now."

Oscar straightened up, looking at her quizzically. "Steve?" he asked.

"No," Jaime said. "Steve's stepfather."

"That's right — he's a pilot. He taught Steve to fly."

"They used to talk about how some day Steve would go to the moon. And he really did it, isn't that amazing? I do remember that . . . boy, were we proud back home in Ojai when the Apollo 17 landed, and there was old Steve walking on the moon!"

They finished gathering the tennis balls and started back to the hospital.

"You trained Steve to be an astronaut, didn't you, Oscar?"

"Well, we've all come a long way since then."

"Yes."

Wrapped in separate thoughts, they entered the building. Oscar turned toward Rudy's office and Jaime headed for her room to pack.

Jim Elgin landed at the airstrip near the village a few hours later and was welcomed by Rudy and Oscar. In a moment, Michael and Jaime arrived in Michael's car and started loading the luggage into the little twin Beech.

"It's nice of you to come and take her home, Jim," Rudy said.

"She's my girl," Jim grinned. "Closest thing to a daughter I ever had, anyway."

"Jim," Rudy spoke quietly, not wanting Jaime to overhear him. But she was off to one side, saying goodbye to Michael. "Jim, Jaime has some blank spots in her memory still. For one thing, and it may be the most important thing, she doesn't remember that she was engaged to marry Steve. She only remembers that they grew up together, that's all."

"I see," Jim said.

"We've been trying to decide how much to tell her about Steve," Oscar added. "About their plans to get married. We're not sure that she's ready to handle the loss of such a serious emotion. It's a pretty important chunk of her life not to remember."

Jim was thinking about his stepson and the girl he loved so much. He wanted to help, to do whatever was best for both of them. "Why don't you let us do it — me and Steve's mother — once Jaime's home and settled a bit?" he suggested.

"I think that's a very good idea," Oscar agreed. They both looked at Rudy, who nodded his approval.

"If she experiences any pain whatsoever, she's to report back here at once," Rudy said. "She knows that."

"Of course," Jim agreed. "The last thing in the world we'd want is to cause her any pain."

Jim shook hands with both men and hopped onto the wing of the plane. Jaime ran over. She kissed Oscar

44

and Rudy. "You guys take care, you hear?" she said.

"We will," they answered in unison. "You, too."

"Thanks again, Jim," Oscar shouted over the warmup sound of the engines.

"My pleasure, Oscar — and don't worry! We'll take care of everything."

Michael helped Jaime into the cockpit. His eyes told her how he felt.

"Michael, you'll always be in my heart."

They kissed, a sweet kiss filled with longing and unexpressed feelings, a kiss without passion that would have to bridge an indeterminate time and an unknowable future.

"Goodbye, Michael."

"Goodbye, Jaime. Take care."

The plane taxied down the runway and soon the waving figures were tiny specks on the ground, then they were out of sight behind the first range of Colorado mountains as the plane headed for the California coast.

No one noticed the lone man in the phone booth just off the airstrip. No one heard him report that the Bonanza was just taking off, that he had checked the flight plan, that they were headed for Ojai, California.

"Excellent," said the crisp voice on the other end of the line. "You know what to do."

"Right," answered the man in the phone booth. "I'll be in touch with you from Ojai, Mr. Harris."

Carlton Harris had a score to settle, and resources that he was keen to match against this particular young woman. He hung up the phone at his end with a smile of satisfaction as well as anticipation.

But the cloudless blue sky seemed to promise clear

45

times ahead as Jaime leaned back to enjoy the flight. The horizon was limitless and she felt that her new life was, too.

"Next stop, Ojai," Jim said.

"Home!" Jaime answered happily.

Chapter Five

A few hours later, they landed at the Santa Monica airport and headed up along the coast to Ventura, then north to Ojai. A sign outside the town proclaimed: "Welcome to Ojai, Home of the American Astronaut, Steve Austin."

"Does Steve still live here?" she asked Jim.

Jim took his eyes off the winding highway to glance at her. She did not seem particularly concerned about the answer, one way or another.

"Well, he's kept pretty busy these days. Doesn't get home too often," Jim answered.

"How beautiful it is," she exclaimed as they drove into the wide quiet streets of the town. "It feels so good to be here."

"Yes," Jim agreed. "Small towns have a warm kind of feel all their own."

"Especially if you grew up here. Even if you don't remember all of it," she said with a smile.

"I remember, though. You and Steve chasing each other through those arches over there." He indicated the row of white adobe shops that lined Main Street. "I met you when you were seven years old."

"Seven..." she repeated. She was busily looking in all directions, at the town square and its park, the shops and winding streets leading off the main tree-lined center. "I've got a lot to catch up on."

"Yes, I guess you do," Jim said. "We want to help you any way we can, Helen and I."

"Of course, I know that. Thank you, Jim."

"No need to thank me. You mean a lot to us."

He headed the car up a narrow residential street that filed through tall palm trees and thick rich desert foliage, until the houses became farther and farther apart and they were almost back in the desert countryside again. He turned in at a small ranch house surrounded by a wide green lawn where cactus and Japanese black pines provided a lush and private aura. As Jim pulled the car to a stop in front of the house, he touched the horn.

A lovely woman in her fifties came running out to greet them. Her arms were open wide to embrace Jaime.

"Welcome home, welcome home, Jaime."

"Thanks...Mom." Jaime returned the hug with a rush of love.

"We were so happy when you called us," Helen said.

"Listen, the way I felt about you and Jim is one of my clearest memories," Jaime said happily as they started up the walk with their arms around each other.

"What about Steve?" Helen joshed.

Jaime stopped in her tracks. "I'm not sure," she said slowly. "There do seem to be some pieces

48

missing.''

Helen was shocked. She hadn't meant to touch any wounds. No one had told her that Jaime was still suffering from some loss of her memory. But—not to remember how she had loved Steve—it was difficult for Helen to understand. Her instincts as a mother and as a woman told her how to handle it. She exuded warmth and love as she led Jaime along to the house. ''The missing pieces will come back, too, with time,'' she said gently.

Jaime was hesitant. ''Maybe...'' she said. She looked around, at the house and its green yard. ''I don't remember this place much. Did I come here a lot?''

Helen laughed. ''No. We just bought it a few months ago.''

''Could've fooled me,'' Jaime said, relieved.

Helen's hand quickened on Jaime's shoulder. The bond of affection between the two women was as strong as it had always been. ''Come on,'' she said, ''I'll show you around.''

Jim started unloading the car, while Helen and Jaime explored around the little ranch house and the large rambling grounds behind it.

''Jim and I are finally going to have time to do some traveling, so we'll be gone quite a lot. But we'd always talked about getting a little farm. We finally decided we'd better do it before we got too old to plow a straight furrow.''

''It'll be a great place to come home to,'' Jaime said sincerely.

''We think so,'' Helen agreed.

''I hope I can find a place nearby that I like,'' Jaime

said.

Helen's eyes sparkled with a secret she was dying to share. "That's part of the reason I brought you out back. Look there!"

Jaime looked in the direction she was pointing. There were two older buildings, which had apparently been the original barn and coach house for the ranch. They were built of fieldstone, simple sturdy buildings with all the delapidated charm of long disuse. Bramble grew up along the walls; the windows covered in years of neglect seemed like dozing eyes of settlers long gone to rest. Those buildings were built to last forever, and their solidity gave Jaime the sense of permanence she so needed now.

"That barn has an apartment over it," Helen was saying.

"It's a wonderful looking place," Jaime exclaimed.

"At least the Health Department might agree to call it an apartment if it were fixed up—a lot," Helen continued. "And with your bionics, that shouldn't be too rough. It's yours if you want it, Jaime."

"Oh, that would be terrific! But . . . I couldn't just—"

"Hey, Jaime, if you really remember how you feel about us, then there's something else you should remember. We're family."

Jaime's eyes felt unaccountably misty. She looked at Helen gratefully. "Right," she said simply. "It's good to be home again, Mom."

"It's good to have you home again. Now," Helen said, clearing her throat which had suddenly gone a little choky, "how about it?"

Jaime looked up at the fine old building drowsing

behind its cover of neglect. Then she grinned. "Well...I'd say you've got yourself a tenant."

There followed a week of frantic activity. Helen had not exaggerated. The apartment over the barn was a real mess. Torn and abandoned furniture, peeling paint, a broken old bicycle, rusted trunks filled with souvenirs of Niagara Falls, washboards, and old Montgomery Ward catalogues, all covered with thick layers of dust. She attacked the windows first, and with a flick of her bionic right hand the grime gave way to sparkling glass, the corroded fixtures were replaced with working locks and sashes, and the accumulation of junk began getting tossed out onto the ground. Nothing was too heavy for her to lift with one hand—Helen stood in amused wonder one morning as an old washing machine came flying through the air and Jaime's cheerful face appeared in the open window a moment later.

"Need any help?" Helen called up to her.

"I'm loving every minute of it!" Jaime answered. "Good workout, too."

"It's hard to believe what I'm seeing," Helen laughed.

"Come on up and watch me scrub the floors," Jaime said. "I figure it should take about ten minutes to get all the sticky guck off, and then scraping the old paint off the walls—do you know, I think there's brick underneath all this plaster?"

"But that's an enormous job!"

"Hey, you're talking to the Bionic Woman! Come on up, I'll show you."

Helen saw, but she still couldn't believe. Jaime's right arm moved faster than the eye could follow. By the end of the day, the brick wall had been exposed and the old paint removed, the floors were scraped and sanded, and all the mess had been tossed onto the junkpile under the window.

"How's this for a finishing touch?" Jaime asked as she ripped the handlebars and seat from the old bicycle, fastened the seat to the center with a twist of her fingers, and hung the result over the door.

"A bull's head—with horns!" Helen laughed. "Jaime, you're a wonder!"

"It's homey, isn't it? I love it, Helen."

Helen glanced around the cozy little apartment. Sunshine flooded through the windows, and everything inside gleamed with promise. Outside, they heard Jim's truck pull up and stop outside the barn. Jaime joined Helen at the window. Jim jumped from the truck's cab and began to struggle with a large white stove strapped to the truckbed.

"I'll be right down to help you," Jaime called. She took the stairs in two jumps. In a moment, she was lifting the heavy stove from the truck with ease, while Jim watched in awe. She carried it carefully up the stairs.

"Hey, the place looks terrific!" Jim said. "It sure didn't take long, did it?"

"Miracle of modern science," Jaime laughed as she set the stove down in its little kitchen alcove.

By the end of the week, everything was connected and Jaime had furnished the apartment with a few second-hand pieces of simple, comfortable things. Now she began to think about the coming autumn, and her work.

While Jaime and the Elgins waited for an answer to

her teaching application, someone else was waiting, too. The ranch was not so isolated that it couldn't be observed by someone really determined to keep an eye on it and its most unusual occupant. If the car that came up their street was frequently the same small white van, no one in the busy and cheerful little ranch noticed. If an occasional helicopter or low-flying private plane seemed to circle low over the house and barn, that wasn't so odd as to be remarked on. Even with her bionic ear, Jaime was not alerted to the sounds of a long-range camera recording her movements. It was a time of peace and settling in for Jaime and renewal of her ''family'' ties, and nothing seemed to threaten the happiness she was beginning to feel.

Chapter Six

One afternoon, when Jim had gone to town, Helen and Jaime were relaxing together in the living room of the ranch house, their feet up and the smell of fresh-baked bread cooling in the kitchen. Jim came in with the mail from the post office, and handed Jaime a letter.

"From the Ojai Public School District," he announced.

"My application!" She slipped her fingernail under the envelope flap and read the letter quickly. Her disappointment was evident. "Now the bad news. Their teaching staff is full."

"Oh, Jaime, I'm so sorry," Helen said.

"Well, Oscar's checking the school at the Air Force base for me. Maybe he'll have better luck," Jaime smiled gamely.

"I hope so," Helen said.

"Now, you mustn't worry about me," Jaime said. "I've weathered worse disappointments, and something will turn up, I'm sure of it."

"Here's a card from Steve—he's in Rome," Jim said. He held the card at arm's length, and then he handed it over to Helen. "Here, you'd better read it. My arms are getting too short."

"Where are your reading glasses?" Jaime asked, ready to get up to look for them.

But Helen was already reading aloud. "Dear Mom and Dad...Rome is beautiful. The people are fun and the food is good, but I still like Mom's 'pasghetti' better. Be home soon. Give Jaime my love, Steve."

"'Pasghetti'?" Jaime repeated.

"That's what he used to call my spaghetti when he was a little boy," Helen said, smiling. "Sure seems like yesterday."

Filled with a passing wave of nostalgia, Steve's mother picked up a scrapbook that was on the library table behind the couch. She opened it to place the postcard inside with a collection of others from all over the world. The book bulged with photographs and clippings.

"Is that a scrapbook? Of Steve?" Jaime asked.

"Yes," Helen answered. She looked up at Jim, worried. Had she touched on a sensitive area again?

"Could I look at it?" Jaime was asking.

She couldn't help noticing Helen's hesitation, and the little silence that fell on the room. "Maybe it'll help me to remember," she explained.

Jim nodded. "Go ahead," he said.

Helen handed the scrapbook to Jaime, and they sat together closely, the book open across their laps. Jim perched on the arm of the couch to look over their shoulders as Jaime turned the pages.

A fading black and white photo of a plump little boy

caught in a moment of rare inactivity. "Oh, is that Steve?" Jaime asked.

"Yes," Helen had to laugh. "He started out a little pudgy, didn't he?"

Jaime nodded. "Yes, but he was cute. Look at this one!"

"There he is with his first fish," Jim said proudly.

"And here's one of you, Jaime," Helen pointed out.

Jaime stared at the solemn-faced little girl of seven or eight. "That's me?"

"Yes, and this one, too."

"Oh, I remember that!" Excitement mounted in Jaime's voice as she turned the pages eagerly.

"And here's one of the two of you together," Helen said. The two teenagers were laughing, their arms casually slung over each other's shoulders. They were both carrying tennis racquets.

Jaime was silent, staring at the picture.

"How much do you remember, Jaime?" Jim asked.

"It's strange. Some of these pictures set off a whole chain of memories, where we were when the camera went off, and how I felt then...and some of the photographs just give me kind of a nice warm general feeling, but at the same time it's as though I were looking at somebody else."

"Look some more," Helen said. She put her arm around Jaime's shoulders.

Steve in a football uniform...a newspaper clipping of herself receiving a tournament cup...the four of them together, in front of the house they used to have...Steve in his Air Force uniform...Steve and Jim on a boat...herself again, on the campus of Carnegie Tech . . . Steve in his astronaut uniform . . .

Jaime felt nothing more than a lively curiosity about this strapping, handsome young man and herself growing up on these pages before her eyes. She did remember, as the scenes passed by, but she felt no more than a sisterly sort of pride at Steve Austin's accomplishments as they began to thicken the album pages with newspaper clippings.

Helen put her hand over Jaime's, to stop her from turning the next page. Jaime looked at her, questioningly.

"Jaime—" It was Jim who spoke. "There's, uh, there's something important you need to know before you turn the next page."

Helen's hand tightened on Jaime's. "You and Steve were much closer than you remember, Jaime," she said gently.

"The next page might be painful for you," Jim went on. His words were like Helen's touch, protective and concerned. Jaime looked up at them, smiled her little half-smile to let them know that she was prepared for whatever it might me, and Helen released her hand. Slowly, Jaime turned the page.

Jaime Sommers to Marry Colonel Steve Austin read the headline. There was a radiant photograph of the two of them, arms around each other, starry-eyed and obviously bursting with happiness.

"What!?" Jaime's voice fell to a whisper as the information slowly sank in. "We were going to be married?"

"Yes."

"We . . . we weren't actually married, were we? Surely I would remember that?"

"No. You became ill just before the wedding. And then..."

"You were very much in love," Jim said.

Jaime was silent, staring at the photograph, reading the story of their plans to be wed in the little church at Ojai. It was dated nearly a year before. She was thunderstruck. "Steve and I..."

"Do you remember anything?" Jim asked anxiously. "Anything at all?"

"So many things..." Jaime murmured, trying to catch at the wisps of memories that darted across the clouds. Riding in a car, an open-top car with the wind blowing through her hair, Steve at the wheel, laughing...eating pizza together...riding horseback...sharing a mission together for Oscar...running in the rain...and alone together on a summer evening, down by the lake...he carved their initials in a tree...they shared a kiss...she saw it all but she felt nothing.

Jim was talking to her, sounding worried. "Is it painful, Jaime? Are you feeling any pain?"

She shook her head, clearing away the images no more real to her than the glossy photographs and newsprint she stared down at. "No," she reassured them, "it's just so hard to believe, to understand. I do remember, some things, little bits of scenes and places where we were together...but it feels like...it feels like there is something missing. Something important."

"What is it, dear?" Helen asked.

Jaime was silent, trying to understand herself, this new self who seemed to have no memory of emotions. "I don't know," she whispered. "I don't know."

"Give it time," Jim said kindly.

"Of course," Jaime sighed. "I'm very grateful for your patience."

"We're just glad to have you back home," Helen said, hugging her. "Now, let's put the past away for a while and concentrate on dinner, what do you say?"

Jaime followed her into the kitchen, and was soon absorbed in the delights of creating a perfect souffle. Life was good, it was marvelous to be alive, and no temporary setback in her job hunt and no sadness for a forgotten love would spoil her determination to live each day as it would come. Long before the table was set, Jim Elgin heard laughter and cheerful voices coming from the kitchen.

The next morning, Jaime was reviewing one of her college textbooks, absorbed in the "new" math, and not unaware of the irony as her bionic fingers turned the pages with barely a ten-thousandth of their potential power, when the ringing of the telephone startled her. It was her first call in the new apartment.

"Jaime?"

"Hello, Oscar, how nice to hear your voice! You're my first caller."

"How's everything going?"

"Well, I struck out with the school here in Ojai," she admitted. "But I'm not discouraged."

"Good, because I think I've found a job for you."

"Oh, Oscar, really? At the Air Force base school?"

"Right. It's only a few miles from you. They've got one teaching position open for this fall, starting immediately."

Jaime reached for a pen and memo pad. "Who do I

talk to?''

''Lieutenant Colonel Tom Hollaway. He's the deputy base commander, and he's expecting your call. I told him about you.''

''All about me?''

''Of course not.''

Jaime laughed. ''That's wonderful, Oscar, I really appreciate it.''

''You haven't got the job yet, but I don't think you'll have any trouble. Oh, by the way, I was talking with Helen earlier this morning. I called the house and she gave me your new number. She tells me that you, uh, found out a few things last night.''

''Yes.''

''Well, uh, how're you feeling?''

''Just fine, Oscar, really.''

''Good. Uh . . . I've got a friend here who'd like to talk to you.'' It wasn't like Oscar to be coy, but Jaime didn't have to wonder long about it. She recognized the other voice immediately.

''Hi.''

''Steve? Hi.'' Jaime settled into the little barrel chair next to the phone. She felt just the slightest bit nervous.

''How're you doing?'' Steve asked. She realized, with a pang, that he felt nervous, too. Somehow, that made her feel better.

''Pretty good,'' she said.

''Mom and Dad okay?''

''Yes, Steve, they're just fine.''

There was a brief awkward pause on the line. ''Will you be coming out this way soon? I know they'd love to see you, Steve.''

"In a couple of days. On my way to Thailand," he answered.

Jaime was a forthright person, and the strain of the polite phone call, she knew, was even rougher on him. After all, he remembered, even if she didn't. She decided to come right out with it. They would have to talk about it sometime. "Can we spend some time together, Steve? I've got a lot to talk to you about."

"Sure," he said. He cleared his throat.

"See you soon, then," she said.

"Yes."

"Bye."

"Bye, Jaime."

They hung up. In Washington, Steve sat quietly for a long moment, wondering. In Ojai, Jaime was doing exactly the same thing.

Chapter Seven

Jaime dressed with special care on the morning of her interview. A skirt instead of her usually neatly pressed jumpsuit, and a bright cherry red blouse and matching sweater, with sensible sandals and her long hair tied back in a thin red ribbon. The drive to the Air Force base was exhilarating. It was her first day out on her own in a long, long time, and the first time she had really felt like herself in longer than she could remember. She was flushed with the wind on her cheeks and her own excitement as she drove up to the main gate.

"I'm Jaime Sommers. I have an appointment with Lieutenant Colonel Tom Holloway at the base school," she said.

The guard checked his roster and waved her on in. She followed the signs and was soon in front of the school building. Colonel Holloway was a handsome young man in his mid-thirties, sandy-haired and blue-eyed. He was delighted to see her and put her at ease immediately.

"Oscar Goldman had a lot of nice things to say about you, Jaime," he told her.

"He's a good friend," she said.

"And I've been a fan of yours myself. I've seen you play tennis a few times. Why did you decide to go back to teaching?"

"I had an accident, skydiving," she said. "And after that, I wasn't . . . quite the same any more." She had rehearsed this with Oscar. Even though she wasn't able yet to remember the accident, it had been reported in the newspapers, and it was a fact. She certainly was not the same! "I've always wanted to teach," she went on seriously, "It was my first love, and now I've decided to settle down."

"I'm afraid you won't get to do much settling with this class," Holloway said. "I've only got one position open, and it's not the easiest. They haven't had a regular teacher in a long time. And they chewed up four substitutes in three months."

"Sounds challenging," Jaime admitted.

"It's a class comprised of sixth, seventh, and eighth graders. They are kids of our service personnel, of course, and they've traveled a lot—which adds to the learning process, but requires a lot of adjusting to new schools, new teachers, new friends. Some of them have tough disciplinarian fathers, who are gone a lot of the time—that sort of thing. You're going to have your hands full. I hope you've got a couple of good solid legs to stand on."

"As a matter of fact, I do."

"Can you start tomorrow?" Holloway asked.

"You bet," Jaime agreed enthusiastically. "Where do I pick up the books?"

"Come on, we'll get them. And—how about a little tennis together some time?"

Jaime smiled back at the colonel and nodded. As they went inside the school building together, she was thinking that she'd have to put in some more time on the practice courts, teaching herself to hold back on the extra power. But this was going to be terrific. Her boss was going to be her friend, and so were those problem kids, if it were humanly—or bionically—possible.

The man in the white van waited outside the base, clocking how much time the target spent inside. He had no way of knowing, yet, what she was doing inside with the Air Force, but it wouldn't be too hard to find out, not with the resources old Mr. Harris had at his command. When Jaime drove out of the gate, the man made a note in his little black book, and followed her to the ranch again at a considerable distance. He didn't have to keep her in sight; the electronics in the back of the van would tell him if she got too far away.

Unsuspecting, Jaime stopped at the little grocery store near home, and then swung on into her own driveway. She was standing at her kitchen table dicing celery into a bowl and reading one of the new textbooks when a knock sounded at her door.

"Come in," she called.

The door opened. "You shouldn't say that without knowing who it is," Helen commented gently as she walked in.

Jaime smiled at her. "Heard your footsteps coming up," she explained. "Bionic ear, you know."

"Oh, of course! I forgot, for a moment."

"Helen, I got the job!"

"Oh, I'm so glad! Have you met your class yet?"

"No. Apparently that's something you have to brace yourself for," Jaime said, laughing.

"Well, I'm sure you'll be able to handle them. How about having dinner with us?"

"Thanks anyway, Mom, but I'm just going to whip up a little tuna salad here. I've got some studying to do." She turned from the table to a kitchen drawer, and rummaged for a minute. "Oh, don't tell me I haven't got a can opener!"

"I'll go back to the house and get you one," Helen said. She started toward the door, but Jaime stopped her.

"No, that's okay! After all, what are fingernails for?"

While Helen watched open-mouthed, Jaime casually dug one of her fingernails into the top of the tunafish can, and worked it around the edge, slicing the tin as a can opener would.

Helen caught her breath. "You haven't got any extra fingernails, have you?" she asked.

"I'll have Rudy check the parts department for you," Jaime promised.

Helen watched the slender young hands as they tossed the salad. She thought about the thing that had amazed her most, ever since she had learned of her son's bionics—that it was not so much the superstrength or even the technological marvel of the replication of nerve and cell and fiber. It was that all appeared to be exactly as nature had intended. No sign set these two apart from the rest of us, no outer sign, at any rate. Helen knew better than anyone what it cost them in emotional adjustments. But the pale pink oval fingernail which she had just seen ripping open a can of

65

tuna now looked too delicate even to be working in a kitchen.

"You're looking thoughtful," Jaime observed.

"Just thinking how glad I am that they didn't spoil your looks, either one of you. I may be prejudiced—although I don't think so—but my two kids, you and Steve, are the handsomest and most beautiful any-where. Jaime...you don't mind my mentioning Steve, do you?"

"Mind? How could I? I've been doing some think-ing about him, too. He'll be home soon."

Helen had been clutching another album, which she put on the table. "I found some more old pictures I thought you might want to see."

"Thank you, Helen. I'll look at them later," Jaime replied.

"It's...not easy, though, is it?"

"No. It's not easy."

"Want to talk about it? How does it feel, Jaime?"

"I look at those pictures, and I see somebody who looks like me, and I remember things, but it's more in my head than in my heart, particularly when I look at Steve. Can I tell you something woman-to-woman, Helen? I care a lot about Steve, but I just don't know where my heart is."

"I understand. Confusion is a frustrating feeling," Helen said.

"It sure is."

"Well, don't be confused about one thing. I almost had you for a daughter-in-law, and nothing would make me happier. But back when you were growing up, and even before you lost your parents, I always thought of you as my daughter, Jaime, and I always will. So I win either way.''

Helen's full heart was suddenly more than she could handle. She leaned over and kissed Jaime's cheek, and then turned and left the apartment. Jaime listened to Helen's receding footsteps idly, not consciously setting off the brain sensors which would activate the microcircuits to instantaneously sensitize her ear to sounds outside the range of normal hearing. It was the desire to hear which set off the supersensitivity, functioning exactly as the human brain does in automatically tuning the body's organs toward receptivity. In ordinary circumstances, here at home with only her foster mother's steps to hear, Jaime's bionic ear was at rest in its perfect disguise as a normal-looking shell of translucent skin and cartilage.

She looked down at the scrapbook. Too much had already been stirred up, too many unresolved thoughts to confuse her. Deliberately, she set the textbook on top of the album. She set a tray for herself next to the easy chair and settled down with her salad and a teacher's manual on classroom techniques.

Chapter Eight

Jaime was the first person to arrive at the base school the next morning, except for a custodian who was sweeping in the hall just outside her classroom.

"Good morning," she said pleasantly, but he only mumbled and moved his broom to show he was busy.

The room was not large, but it was airy and functional. Twenty desks were lined up facing the teacher's podium. There was a good-sized blackboard on an easel, an old-fashioned army surplus number on wheels which had probably seen plenty of service in military briefing sessions. Jaime set her books down on the teacher's desk and took up the notes she had spent hours preparing the night before. She began to cover the blackboard with three columns, headed "6th," "7th," and "8th"—introductory assignments for each segment of her group.

Happy with the smell of chalk and the feeling of being in a schoolroom again, Jaime became totally absorbed in her work. By the time she finished, the blackboard was covered with her small, neat printing, and she looked up to see children crossing the wide yard outside the window. There were sounds of footsteps and voices out in the hall. She stepped outside her room.

Children of all ages were coming through the outer door, some reluctant and some eager, in the way of children all over the world. A sullen-faced girl of about twelve stopped, sized Jaime up, and sidled past her into the classroom. Two or three others followed, some returning her "good morning" and some simply staring and brushing past her.

An attractive young woman about Jaime's own age came out of the classroom across the hall.

"Hi," she said. "You're Jaime!"

"Right." Jaime smiled.

"Welcome aboard. I'm Karen Stone."

"Hi, Karen."

"I was new here last year, but now I'm an old hand, so if you need any help, just holler."

"Thanks. Thanks very much."

"And you may need it sooner than you think." Karen nodded toward Jaime's room. "You know that they gave you the 'dirty dozen,' huh?"

"I heard," Jaime said. "Are they really all that bad?"

Karen's smile was encouraging. "Aw, not really," she said. "They're into pre-adolescence, and so they're a little more outspoken than some of the older classes. And, of course, you're a new teacher, and you've got to be put through the mill."

Jaime nodded thoughtfully. She had to duck just then as a freckled, snub-nosed little girl in a tie-dyed jumper dashed past them into the room, almost knocking Jaime down. Karen Stone waved in a "good luck" gesture, and went inside her own classroom, closing the door behind her. All that remained in the hallway were two teenage boys, leaning against a water fountain, and Jaime.

"Are you in my class?"

The younger boy nodded. The other just stared.

"Well, come on, then," Jaime said cheerfully, and turned to go inside. The boys deliberately stayed behind for a moment or two, but as soon as she had closed the door, they opened it again and came into the room. The class was very noisy, laughing and talking.

The bell rang just as Jaime took her seat. The class waited for her to speak. But there was still a strong undercurrent of giggling and poking going on. Their faces were curious, cynical, sarcastic, hostile, mischievous, or just plain bored. Suddenly, she felt nervous.

"Well," she said brightly. "Good morning. I'm Miss Sommers."

"We know it!" a boy's voice rang out from the back row.

Well, you can't say nobody warned you, Jaime told herself silently. Here we go!

"Well, that's good," she said, smiling her sunniest smile. "I'll get to know all of your names as quickly as I can."

"You had to quit tennis, huh?" It was a gum-chewing girl of about thirteen, slouched back in her chair.

The only way Jaime knew how to deal with people was directly and honestly.

"That is kind of a long story," she said, "and I'll

tell you sometime, when we get to know each other better. Now, I don't know what routine you've been used to, but I've put my plans for the classroom organization up on the board here—''

The class seemed agitated with an attack of the titters as she turned to point to the blackboard on which she had spent the previous hour. It had been erased.

As she stared at it, the kids broke into real guffaws.

''Well. I thought I had put the plans up on the board,''Jaime said. She turned her back to them without a trace of the annoyance they were expecting. ''Excuse me a moment,'' she said.

She turned the large easel frame on its casters so that it was facing the other way, and stepped behind it. Picking up the chalk with her right hand, she rewrote the material at bionic speed. The class couldn't see what she was doing, and the tittering grew louder and more excited. In less than a minute, Jaime turned the blackboard around again, and the children gasped. The entire assignment had been neatly replaced.

''How'd she do that so fast?'' whispered a girl in the middle of a row, giving herself away as the guilty—and disappointed—culprit. Jaime made no sign that anything unusual had occurred.

''Now then,'' she went on, ''I'd like you each to copy off the section that applies to you—sixth, seventh, or eighth grade.''

When she turned again to point to the board, a fast-moving pellet hit her in the back. She winced, then bent to pick up the spitball.

''Who did that?'' she asked quietly, but of course there was no evidence of the rubberband weapon in sight. Only a sea of faces waiting to see what she

71

would do.

She couldn't ignore that. She looked over the kids, and then indicated a gawky young boy seated at a desk near the bookcase.

"Would you hand me that telephone book over there, please? No, the big one. That's it. Thank you." The boy handed her the book, a directory of the main Los Angeles area, about four inches thick. Holding it between her two hands in front of her, where all the children could see it plainly, she spoke in a calm, deceptively casual voice.

"I guess you all know what a reputation this class had. The other teachers have all kinds of terrific names for you. I hear that you can be a rough and rowdy bunch. Well, that part doesn't bother me, because that tells me you've got a lot of spirit, and I like that." These kids had heard that before, and she had lost some of her audience. Apathy and barely suppressed groans greeted what they anticipated as another boring lecture. But Jaime wasn't worried about that. She knew how to get their attention. She went on in the same quiet voice.

"But I'm not just another substitute. I'm here to stay, and if we're going to get along, you are going to have to learn a little about respect, too. Now, some teachers feel that the best way to get respect is to threaten their kids."

Bored eyes turned to staring ones, small spines were bolted upright from their slumped positions, and jeering mouths were opening in wonder as she spoke. It wasn't what she was saying so much as the fact that she was ripping the Los Angeles phone book in half while she spoke.

"Now, I don't like to make threats," she was saying, "because so many times, they're just not carried out. I've always felt that the gentle approach is the best one."

Jaime held the heavy phone book in front of her with her left hand, while her right hand slowly pulled upward, tearing the thick mass of pages right up the center. Her voice was easy and natural, as if unaware of what her hands were up to. The children began to tune in carefully to what she was saying.

"I feel that respect for a teacher should grow naturally, out of friendship and trust," she went on. "I certainly expect you to understand and to develop that sort of respect for me."

The reactions of some of the individual students tipped her off as she watched them staring and squirming in their seats. She thought she could spot the person who had erased the board and singled out the uncomfortable little boy who had performed so accurately with his slingshot. He was the one who was leaning forward to whisper in his neighbor's ear. Jaime decided to listen in.

"Boy, this broad is spooky!" the boy whispered in a shaky breath.

"I'll make you a deal," Jaime announced, looking straight at him. "I won't call you a service brat, and you don't call me a broad."

All the other children turned to stare at Teddy, who blushed a deep scarlet and murmured strictly to himself, "Wow, how'd she hear that?"

"I've got very good hearing," Jaime said.

The other children were silent as they turned to face front.

Jaime felt relaxed and in control now. She had the children's attention and a certain respect. Now she would tackle the hard part—teaching.

"Let's break up this regimentation a little bit," she said. "Why don't we start by pushing the desks into a circle so we can all see each other, huh?" The class sat quietly, not sure of what to expect.

"Once we get the desks moved, I want each of you to write a biography of yourself. I want to know all there is to know about you, each one of you. So think about that while you're moving the desks. Well? C'mon, let's go!"

The children began to react, slowly. First one, then another and soon all of them rose and began to push the desks into a large circle which included the teacher's stand. Jaime felt them watching her cautiously, but her pleasant smile reassured them that the new teacher had a lot more surprises in store for them and that this was going to be an interesting semester indeed.

Chapter Nine

Lieutenant Colonel Holloway met her as she was coming out of the school building at the end of the day. He called to her as she was heading for her car.

"Miss Sommers! Uh . . . Jaime? How was your first day?"

"Fun," she replied, with a wide grin.

"I'm sure you'll do fine," he said. "Listen, the control tower just called my office with a message for you. Colonel Austin radioed that he was over San Antonio and should be landing here in an hour and a half."

Jaime opened the door of her car and slid in. "Good," she said. "I'll come back in time to meet him."

Tom Holloway remembered something about Jaime Sommers and Steve Austin being engaged, and it crossed his mind that she was being awfully casual about meeting her fiance.

"Uh, are you . . ."

Jaime waited, looking up at him.

"Are, uh, you and he, uh . . ."

She understood, and answered him candidly. "I'm not really sure, Tom," she said.

He grinned down at her. He had a dimple in his chin. "Just checking. Okay?"

"Sure," she smiled, and started the car. She waved to him and drove off toward the main gate.

A black Mustang which had been parked outside the gate, hidden by a bend in the road, now gunned its motor and pulled out in the same direction she had gone.

The road back to Ojai wound through woods and foothill country. It was generally a secluded area, before the country road turned into a real highway near town. Jaime enjoyed the quiet and solitude of the drive. A car passed her and sped recklessly ahead, rounding the curves to roar out of her sight. Jaime shook her head, wondering how people could be so careless with their lives, so oblivious to the dangers of the road and the beauties of the world around them.

Steve was coming, and they had so much to talk about. She thought about what they would say to each other, how much she might be prompted to remember, whether all of her recent past would return to her, whether her feelings—

Her thoughts were interrupted by a screeching of brakes just ahead of her. She watched in horror as the black Mustang which had sped past her now swerved to avoid another car approaching at an intersection. Before her foot even had time to step on her own brakes, the two cars ahead of her collided with an ear-shattering crash.

She slowed and stopped at the side of the road. The

driver who had run the intersection now reversed his car in a shriek of rubber and pulled away. He zoomed out of sight over the hill.

The Mustang was nowhere in sight. She ran to the site of the collision, where dust and smoke was beginning to rise from a deep gulley below the road.

The car was half on its side in the dirt. She ran down the gulley, slipping and sliding on the incline. The smoke was thick, and as she approached the car she saw fingers of flame begin to jab forth from the steaming hood. Behind the shattered windshield, she saw a man's panicky face.

"Help! Please help me! It's going to explode!"

Jaime pulled at the car door, but it was bent and jammed shut.

"Help! The fire is spreading!" the man called hysterically. The smoke was thickening and the flames danced higher. There was an acrid smell of burning oil.

"My legs—I can't move!"

Without hesitating, Jaime grabbed the bent steel door of the Mustang with her right hand, and using all her bionic strength she ripped it from its frame. It came away slowly, but finally it was free. She tossed it aside, and leaned down to help the driver out.

The steering wheel seemed to be pinning him in. He gasped helplessly. Jaime reached in, gripped the steering column firmly, and bent it out of his way. Then she pulled him from the car. She dragged his limp and overweight body to a safe distance about five yards from the smouldering wreck. Just as she stopped to catch her breath, there was a deafening roar, and flames engulfed the Mustang in a huge ball of fire.

The driver seemed only semiconscious.

"Can you walk?" Jaime asked him.

"No . . . the pain! Don't move me."

"All right," she said. "You stay here. Don't try to move. I'll be back with help as soon as I can."

The man forced a smile of gratitude, and his eyes closed. He sank back against the pine brush. Jaime ran up the side of the gulley in two or three bionic steps, and ran to her car.

She was unaware that the man's eyes, alert and not the least bit dazed, followed her until she was out of sight.

Chapter Ten

It was only a half hour later when Jaime returned to the scene of the wreck. She was followed by a rescue vehicle with its siren going full-blast. She stopped her car and ran to the side of the gulley, where black smoke still poured forth in an ominous column.

"This way, quickly," she said to the ambulance attendants. "He's right down—"

But he wasn't. The car was there, still burning. The fire team began instantly to hose it down. But there was no sign of the accident victim in the clearing where she had left him.

She edged her way around the wreck and walked all around the area of the clearing. Broken pine scrub and clear marks in the dirt showed that she was not mistaken, but the man was nowhere around.

"You're sure this was where you left him?"

There was no place for anyone to hide there, with the sparse trees and cactus ground cover. It was clear that the rescue team and Jaime Sommers were the only persons anywhere near that gulley right now.

"He *was* here," Jaime could only say, bewildered.

"Maybe somebody came by and saw him and took him to the hospital," the highway patrolman suggested.

"No . . . he said he couldn't be moved," Jaime said. Her clear brow contracted in a puzzled frown.

"Then where is he?" the ambulance attendant asked reasonably. He stared at Jaime, as if wondering what she was up to.

"I don't know," she said.

"Let's get out of here, then," the attendant said. He turned to scramble up the side of the gulley, and the others followed. The highway cop took Jaime's arm, and for a wild second she thought she was being arrested—for a false alarm, maybe, a hoax? No, that was absurd. The cop was only helping her up the steep incline. When they reached the road, he told the ambulance men to go on back to town, and assured Jaime that he would file a report and check out the hospital. "He'll probably turn up in the emergency ward," he said. "If we need you for anything, we'll call you."

"Okay," Jaime said. She looked back over her shoulder to the smouldering, empty slope.

"The fire's out, and the wrecking tow will be here pretty soon," the policeman said.

"And I've got to meet a plane," Jaime remembered suddenly, looking at her watch.

"Run along, then, and thanks for your help," the cop said.

"Thank you," she replied. "For a minute there, I wasn't sure I hadn't made the whole thing up."

"Oh, there was a wreck all right, and you did the right thing. The victim will turn up." The patrolman got back into his car.

Jaime drove back to the base slowly. There was still plenty of time before Steve's plane came in, but this time she wasn't enjoying the scenery. She was mystified and confused. Was there still something wrong with her head? But no, the cop believed her. It was just a little odd, that's all. Except... the man had been so helpless, and in pain. How could he have moved—or been moved—from that spot?

The accident had occurred at the intersection near town, and by the time Jaime reached the base again, she figured that the police had had time to check the hospital. She went directly to a phone booth near the landing strip, and put in a call to the highway patrol.

After a brief conversation, her puzzlement was deeper than ever. She sat for a moment and then dialed the number Oscar had given her. He had urged her to report anything the least bit strange that happened. She felt slightly foolish calling him about this, but... she was put directly through to Oscar, and his steady calm voice reassured her immediately. She told him what had happened on the road.

"...and they still haven't found any trace of him, Oscar. It was the strangest thing..."

"I'll look into it," Oscar promised. "And, Jaime, let me know if anything else unusual happens. Anything at all."

"Okay. Listen, I've got to run—there's Steve's plane landing now. Thanks, Oscar, and see you soon? Good. Bye..."

She hung up, her attention completely taken by the sight of an F-104 reversing its jet engines and swooping to a thunderous landing.

In a few minutes, Steve had climbed down from the cockpit and strode toward her with a giant smile on his broad tan face. They didn't embrace, but she was sure that she was just as glad to see him as his smile told her he was to be there. After he had checked in with the central tower, they got into her car and drove to Ojai. Helen and Jim were waiting.

As she drove past the scene of the accident, Jaime merely glanced toward the gulley but said nothing to Steve about her experience. The smoke had died away and there was nothing to be seen from the road. It was as if it had never happened.

They talked about Steve's parents, about the ranch and Jaime's delight in her new apartment over the barn. They talked of Steve's recent trips and how good it would be to settle in with a heaping plate of Helen's spaghetti when they got home. She told him about her new job, and what had transpired in the classroom that morning. They talked of the countryside and the sunshine. They talked of everything except what was most on both their minds.

Dinner was a warm and cheerful family affair. Jaime felt easier with Steve as the hours went by. When he said goodnight, he asked if she'd like to join him in a long walk around Ojai the next day, after school. She remembered, with a rush of pleasure, what it felt like to be an attractive young woman looking forward to a date with someone who might turn out to be special.

Her thoughts that night as she drifted off to a dreamless sleep were not about cars careening off the road, or mysteriously disappearing strangers, or even a roomful of bright-eyed kids responsive to her eagerness to reach them. She was thinking about tomorrow.

And what a lovely day it turned out to be. The sun cast a clear, soft brightness over the clean white streets and green parks of Ojai. Steve and Jaime strolled through the town, avoiding the arcaded Main Street with its shadowy trees and well-meaning citizens who would stop them for a handshake and a friendly word. Steve Austin was a celebrity in his home town, not only because he had been an astronaut, but because so many people there remembered him as a lively little boy, a high school football star, and a bright kid, a little on the wild side, whom everybody knew would turn out all right. People liked to chat with him on his rare visits home and he enjoyed it, too, most of the time. But today he and Jaime walked the sleepy sidestreets and stayed clear of chance meetings that would cut into their brief time together. They had too much to find out about each other, too little time to spend testing the currents between them for sparks.

They walked past the library, and the old Methodist church, and past the schoolhouse to the deserted playground behind it. Most of the children had gone off—to their music lessons or to race their skateboards or to gather at someone's backyard pool for a splash party before the warm afternoon sun would suddenly give way to the mountain chill of evening.

"It feels good to be back in Ojai," Jaime said as they crossed the softball diamond.

"Even if you don't remember all of it?" Steve asked.

"Even then," she answered. "You know, I saw your mom's old scrapbook. We really did grow up together, huh?"

"Yes. Do you remember any of it?"

"Bits and pieces. I've really been trying to . . . how did we meet the first time?"

Steve chuckled. "It was my first day in the third grade. You dared me to eat one of everything in the cafeteria."

"Did I?" No image fell into place in Jaime's memory, but not everybody remembered everything about their childhoods. She was mostly curious about what kind of kids they had been. "Did you do it?"

"I tried," Steve remembered with a rueful smile, "and got pretty sick." He looked down at her, but she shook her head. Nothing.

"I got back at you, though," he said. They had reached the swings, and he grabbed the chain on the first one. "Right here on this swing."

"What'd you do? Put a frog down my back?" she laughed.

"A lizard," Steve said.

She shivered in mock horror. "What a rotten thing to do!"

Steve sat down on the swing. Impulsively, Jaime gave him a push—with her right hand. The surge of her bionic force sent Steve's two hundred pounds of muscle and brawn soaring high up, higher and higher, and then up over the top pole of the frame that held the row of swings. He did a complete loop, hanging on for dear life.

"Hey!" he shouted, taken by surprise.

Jaime shielded her eyes against the bright sun to look up at him as he swung almost over again on the second revolution. She felt like an impish little girl again, and the laughter welled up inside her with a nostalgic mix of triumph and tease. That would teach him to put lizards down people's backs! As the sun blurred her vision of the grown man flying up in a free arc, she unexpectedly saw a little boy there instead. Dark-haired, scruffy, laughing and playing rough, but somehow she knew he would protect her if she ever got into real trouble, too.

The swing's trajectory slowed, and she saw that it was not the boy, but the man now. Heartened by the memory, and somewhat saddened by it, too, she said nothing. He took her hand as they walked on across the playground.

"There's the lake, down there beyond that row of trees. Do you remember?" he asked her. Jaime shook her head, as if to clear the vision.

"I'm not sure," she said.

But she seemed to be leading the way, and when they got to the bank of the little lake, he let her set the pace. She stopped at a certain tree. Her hand reached up to touch a carved heart.

Steve said nothing. He looked over her shoulder at the slender fingers as they traced the outline, and the words *Jaime and Steve* cut inside it.

"Why did you hide this from me before?" she asked.

"Let's sit down, here on the grass," he said. "Look, Jaime, the operation to make you bionic was my idea. It was the only way to save you from—well, either dying or being a cripple all your life. But your reaction to the bionics was different from mine. When your body started to reject the implants, you suffered terrible pains, especially when you were reminded of the past—of what we had been to each other or even your childhood here in Ojai. The pain seemed directly attached to the memories, so . . . well, I just didn't want you suffering any more. But now you're really well—''

''But some parts of my memory are still missing,'' she finished for him. ''There isn't any pain any more, Steve. Now I can face what we were to each other, that we were going to be married.''

''You know?''

She nodded. ''It must have been awful for you, Steve, having to keep it all bottled up inside you.''

The dappled light filtered through the oak tree's wide branches. There was a stillness in the air, as if all the world had gone quiet, waiting for time to catch up. Steve's wide-set eyes caught sparks from the sun that danced across his face. He waited, aching to touch Jaime's cheek. He felt a whirling galaxy of emotions, and the strongest was his fear of hurting her again.

Jaime sighed, a tender little sound that broke the quiet as softly as a leaf falling to the ground.

''Steve, can you understand how mixed up I feel? I can appreciate all that you've done for me, and everything we must have shared together, but I just don't . . . I don't feel those emotions now, Steve. I don't remember what it's like to be in love with you.''

His voice was hoarse with unsaid words. ''I understand,'' was all he could manage, and then he had to look away from her.

Jaime reached out to put her hand on his arm. ''But I do know this, Steve . . . you're a wonderful man, and noble—'' She saw his jaw tighten, and she smiled a little. ''And from the pictures I saw, you were an awfully cute third grader. A little pudgy, but cute.''

She was rewarded with the hint of a smile from him, a visible relaxing of the taut line of his averted jaw. ''I can understand how we got to be so close,'' she went on softly. ''Maybe we'll be that close again, even closer, in time. Can you give me some time, Steve? Can this be a new beginning for us?''

Steve looked at her, finally, but he had no words. He had joked and talked of romantic things with lots of women before, and he was far from being a schoolboy in matters of the heart. But this woman meant more to him than any ever had, and losing her this way was even harder to handle than if she had really died on the operating table. He was grateful that she was alive and well and more beautiful than ever, that she could share his isolation as a bionic being, that she could understand, and that they had once shared so much. And that they might again. That was what he would cling to. He was supposed to be a very brave fellow. This was somehow harder than climbing into the cockpit of an untried rocket plane.

But he loved her enough to wait, and hope. He took her hand. He couldn't quite manage to speak, but his answer was in his eyes. They would wait out however much time it took, separately and together. He would go his way, doing missions for Oscar and that bunch, and Jaime would stay here and try to get back her heritage of memories. And when she did—if she did—well, they had that to look forward to.

The shadows had lengthened as they sat there, and the warmth of the afternoon was gone. Jaime and Steve rose from the lakeside and walked away from the carved old tree. They were comfortable together now, and easy.

Jaime's right hand and Steve's left were entwined as they walked. They looked like any normal couple hurrying home in the early twilight. The touch of their hands felt to them exactly as it felt to millions of other young couples who were getting to know each other.

Oscar Goldman would have been gratified to observe how nearly perfect his bionic experiments were working.

Chapter Eleven

High on a crest overlooking the blue Pacific Ocean, Carlton Harris leaned back in his leather chair and looked across the wide polished mahogany desk at the man who was talking so excitedly to him.

"You wouldn't have believed what she did to get me out of that car after Johnny hit me, Mister Harris," the man repeated.

"Oh, I'd believe it all right, Sayers. I got the video tape you sent. Would you like to watch a replay?"

"Sure, Mister Harris." Sayers had the rough-and-ready look of an ex-Hollywood stunt man, which he was, and the hungry expression of a guy who would do absolutely anything for money. Harris found him distasteful, but useful.

He flipped the switch on the video monitor, and the road between Ojai and the Air Force base came onto the little screen. The two men watched in fascinated silence as the Mustang passed Jaime Sommers' car and then crashed into the oncoming car at the intersection. The camera's long-range lens zoomed in on Jaime as she ran from her car to the gulley, wrenched open the bent steel door, and dragged Sayers to safety. It lingered on her as she ran back up the gulley at bionic speed, and then the picture faded out and the screen was dark.

"Yes, Miss Sommers is quite a unique young woman, in more ways than one. I think it's time I went to Ojai," Harris mused, more to himself than to Sayers. But he looked up, smiling. "We have quite a few surprises in store for her."

"Yes, sir, Mister Harris," Sayers responded eagerly.

"Don't be so anxious," Harris said without troubling to hide his disdain. "This will require a certain finesse. I want you to do nothing until I specifically order you to. Do you understand?"

"Oh, sure, sure."

"She got away from me once before, and now that we've found her again, nothing must go wrong."

"I wasn't even there when she and that guy broke into the refinery," Sayers protested.

"Exactly. That is why you are here now and why the gentlemen who worked for me before are not."

"I get it."

"Good."

Harris pushed the control button to begin the tape again, and dismissed Sayers with a wave of his hand as he leaned forward to study the film.

Oscar Goldman was at the house when Steve and Jaime came back from their walk. Steve was needed immediately; a jet was warming up at the base ready to take him to Thailand. For once, Steve was almost relieved to be leaving on a mission. It would take his mind off other things.

"How long will you be gone this time?" Helen asked, when they walked out to say goodbye at the front gate.

Steve kissed his mother. "Just until I can convince Oscar that the mission is completed," he said.

"Which won't be long, knowing you," Oscar answered wryly.

"Well, the sooner he's home again, the better we'll all like it," Jim said.

"You coming, Oscar?"

"Not right away, Steve. I've got some business to settle here."

Steve got into the car. Jaime leaned down to the window.

"You will come back home to see me, won't you?"

"You can count on it," he answered. They shared a last lingering look, and then a kiss.

Jaime stepped back, and Steve drove off with a wave of his hand.

"So long, son . . . be careful . . . bye . . ." Helen and Jim, their arms around each other, turned toward the house.

"How about some spaghetti, Oscar? Steve's favorite," Helen said.

"I'd love it," Oscar answered. "Jaime and I will join you two in a minute."

"What's wrong, Oscar?" Jaime asked as soon as they were alone.

Oscar looked stern. "Jaime," he said, "I'm concerned about something."

"I can see that. What is it?"

"It may be dangerous for you to stay here in Ojai."

Jaime's gray eyes opened wide. It wasn't like Oscar to overstate something. But how could this place be dangerous—it was the most peaceful setting she could imagine.

"Dangerous! What are you talking about?"

"That auto accident you came across—it may not have been an accident at all. Someone may be trying to kill you."

"What? Who?"

"We don't know." Oscar was speaking calmly, in his driest and most matter-of-fact tone. "At any rate, we don't feel it's safe for you to stay here. So I want you to plan—"

She interrupted him. "Now wait a minute, Oscar. I came back to Ojai to put down some roots. To teach. To make a whole new life. I'm not going to run away from all of that just because you're suspicious."

Oscar nodded. This was what he had expected her to say. "But what if the next time there's an 'accident,' you're caught right in the middle of it yourself. Are you really ready for that?"

"Yes," she said quickly. Then she had to smile. Her smile was one of Jaime's most endearing features. It curved easily and just the slightest bit crookedly with a hint of the minx she had once been. But her eyes gave her away. They were solemn, flashing deep and thoughtful response to his words. Oscar knew he had made his point, even when she went on to say, "I guess that's easy for me to say, huh?"

"Yeah," he replied laconically.

"But I've got to stay, Oscar. Sooner or later I've got to take a stand for myself. It might as well be now." She gestured toward the house. "You go on in. I'll be there in a minute." She leaned forward and kissed his cheek. "And don't worry. I'll do just fine."

Oscar nodded. He turned to go in the house. Jaime stayed there, on the edge of the property near the road, gazing out across the countryside and thinking about what he had said.

She owed her life to Oscar, and she wanted to repay him any way she could. If he said she was in danger, she knew that it was not an idle speculation. But this was one order—or suggestion—that she could not follow. Whatever her special fate was to be, wherever her bionic qualifications led her into work for the OSI, Jaime knew that her own identity was the foundation without which nothing would be possible. She was just starting to build that foundation, and it looked like it was going to be pretty solid. She would stay in Ojai, work with those feisty, marvelous kids and teach them something. She would cement her family relationships, and maybe someday . . . but whatever came, she felt ready for the challenge.

As she turned to follow Oscar into the house, a large black limousine moved slowly along the road toward the ranch. The windows were heavily tinted so that no one could see in. But Carlton Harris could see out. As his driver passed the retreating figure of the tall, lithe young woman, Harris's mouth turned inward in a satisfied grin of anticipation.

Chapter Twelve

"Why weren't there any women's signatures on the Declaration of Independence?" asked the red-headed girl named Gwen. She was the same one who had erased the blackboard on Jaime's first day.

"Now, that's a good question. Who's got an answer?" Several hands went up eagerly. The class was seated in a circle, all the desks facing each other. Jaime looked around the circle, and chose one. "Joey?"

"Well, no woman signed the Declaration of Independence 'cause it was harder for a woman to get a good education back then."

"There'd be a lot of women signers nowadays," Gwen said thoughtfully.

"You've come a long way, baby," tow-headed Teddy commented with his usual surplus of verbal energy.

The class laughed, and so did Jaime. The bell rang.

"Okay, gang," Jaime said. "Read Chapter Four tonight, and tomorrow we'll set up our own Continental Congress. See ya."

"Bye, Miss Sommers...see you tomorrow...give me liberty or give me death..." the children chorused cheerfully as they scrambled to get out into the sun.

Jaime gathered her papers and headed for the parking lot. As she drove along the winding country road, she found her thoughts wandering back to the accident, still unexplained and now a vague spectre in the back of her mind. To distract her thoughts, she turned on the radio.

"...so the situation in the Far East seems to be stabilizing. And in Thailand, American astronaut Steve Austin was given a royal welcome by the king, who is an amateur astronomer and space buff..."

Jaime smiled. The wind blew her long hair freely behind her as the little car wound up the hill and began the steep descent.

A loud explosion cracked the air. It came from under the car, and rocked the chassis violently. The radio burst into loud static, and she shut it off quickly. She put her foot down hard on the brake.

Nothing happened. The car was accelerating as it gathered momentum on the downward grade. She felt her control slipping. She pumped the brake several times, but nothing happened. The brakes were completely gone.

The car careened down the hill, and it was all Jaime could do to keep it on the right side of the blacktop road. She maneuvered with both hands and kept her foot down on the useless, dead brake.

A sharp hairpin curve was ahead. Jaime's eyes widened with near-panic as she saw something looming across the road in front of her. A giant log was lying across the pathway, and she was approaching it

95

at a deadly speed.

She opened the door of the car. Her bionic foot left the brake and hit the blacktop. Using her foot like a brake, she dragged against the speeding car with an intense effort. A thin screeching sound rose from the contact of her shoe against the road. Smoke from her burning shoe rose and filled her flared nostrils with a sharp, unpleasant scorching odor. But the car was slowing, and Jaime's bionic foot was feeling no pain.

The car rolled to a stop inches from the log.

Shaken, relieved, Jaime sat for a moment in the sudden quiet, catching her breath. She looked down at her shoe. It had completely burned away, nothing remaining but the top strap and a flimsy black ash.

Her bionic ear picked up the sound of a motor starting and a car driving away. Puzzled, she listened until it was out of range. Then she got out of her car, locked it, and began a barefoot walk into town.

By the time she reached the ranch, she was more angry than upset. "Y'know what makes me the maddest?" she said to Helen. "That was my favorite pair of shoes."

"Jaime, cut the kidding. You could have really been hurt."

"Yeah, well, accidents happen."

"Are you sure it was an accident?" Helen asked pointedly.

"Now, now," Jaime smiled. "You aren't going to pull that worried mother stuff after all this time, are you?"

"Jaime . . . Oscar called a little while ago. He said he was coming tomorrow. And the very first thing he asked was if you were all right. He sounded worried."

"Oh, Helen, have you ever known Oscar not to sound worried?" Then, seeing that Helen was seriously concerned, Jaime relented. "Okay, okay. I'll call him." She kissed Helen as she passed her to go to the phone.

Before her finger reached the dial, her right ear picked up a signal—a click, inaudible, probably, to anyone else, but loud and clear to her. I must be on the alert for danger now, she realized, as she listened to the telltale electronic hum that followed the switch-on.

"What is it, dear?" Helen asked.

Jaime set the phone back on its hook. Then she said, "I don't know. Do me a favor, will you? Call Oscar on your phone, and tell him to hurry out here. Something strange *is* going on."

Helen hurried out to make the call. But Oscar was not to be found immediately. The urgent message was relayed to him, and when he returned the call later that night, he assured Jaime he would be there the next day.

"I'll be at school," Jaime told him. "Can you meet me there?"

"Maybe you'd better not go to work tomorrow," Oscar said.

After a beat, Jaime said seriously, "Maybe I'd better, Oscar."

It was mid-afternoon and her class had already been dismissed by the time Oscar showed up. Jaime was sitting at her desk, trying to concentrate on correcting papers in the empty classroom.

She was startled when a voice spoke her name.

"Miss Sommers?"

She looked up and smiled to see a little boy in splattered and damp jeans, standing in the doorway with a look of satisfied effort on his round face.

"Hi, Teddy."

"The washtub's all cleaned up," he reported.

"Terrific. You wouldn't want people dunking for apples in a dirty tub," she said.

"Right. Hey, are you gonna come to the fair tomorrow?"

A man in a dark business suit loomed up in the doorway behind Teddy, and her feeling of relief told Jaime how tense she had been all day. She glanced past Teddy to Oscar, nodded, and then returned her full attention to the boy.

"I'm sure going to try to get there," she answered. "You have a nice weekend, okay?"

"Yeah," Teddy said. "You, too, Miss Sommers."

"Thank you, Teddy."

Oscar came in, closing the door behind him.

"Well?" Jaime asked. She was biting the eraser tip of her pencil.

"We did a thorough check on your car. The garage said it looked like the brake line had been rigged with a small charge."

"So it really wasn't an accident."

"No, it wasn't. And you were right about your phone. It is tapped."

"By whom?"

"We've traced two men to this town. They may have you under surveillance. Does the name Carlton Harris mean anything to you?"

Jaime answered without hesitation. "Yes—the so-called lady-killer who owned the Caribbean oil refinery that Steve and I tried to break into..."

The jigsaw puzzle of her memory was complete

now, except for a few missing pieces near the heart of it—the ones having to do with her feelings for Steve. She remembered things they did together, and she remembered how, after the skydiving accident, when she first became bionic, she and Steve had gone on a mission together. It was unfinished business— unfinished because her bionics had failed her and she had almost blown it for both of them.

"That's right, Jaime. But Carlton Harris has a lot more going for him than just that refinery. He owns a vast conglomerate of many companies. We've even discovered that one of his companies was awarded a government contract recently."

"Well, then, which is he? A good guy or a bad guy?" Jaime began collecting her papers, and Oscar helped her to straighten the schoolroom as they talked.

"He's a very bad guy, Jaime, but we've never been able to prove it. That was the purpose of your original mission, if you recall..."

Oscar watched her without seeming to and busied himself straightening pencils and chalk while Jaime's mind raced back to the dark night when she and Steve stood outside a mammoth refinery, high on a hill overlooking an endless network of pipes and valves and tanks and busy workmen. With his bionic eye, Steve had spotted Carlton Harris, and described him to Jaime.

"Well dressed, obviously rich. Carries himself like he owns the world—well, I guess he does...this part of it, anyway. What a spread!"

"What's he doing, Steve?"

"Talking to someone, a guy in army fatigues, looks like a gorilla—wait, they're walking over to one of the tanks. Jaime, he's pointing to something ... looks like some kind of relay switch. Can you hear what they're saying?''

Jaime had concentrated on the direction of the two tiny specks Steve pointed to. Her ear picked up their voices, faint but clear as she zeroed in.

''He's talking about security precautions. There's a switch just like this one in the main control room of the refinery ... and they're connected in series ... the only way anyone can gain entrance to the vault and the munitions—munitions!—will be by turning both switches simultaneously ... otherwise the booby trap charges in the door will blow up in their faces. My gosh, Steve,'' she said, turning back to him, ''how are we going to get in there without getting blown up at the front door?''

''I'll have to get to the control room somehow and throw that switch while you trip the one down there on the tank.''

But Jaime had insisted that Harris's reputation as a ladies' man (''lady-killer,'' Steve reminded her grimly) would play right into their hands. She would pretend to be a newspaper reporter, flirt a little with Harris, and get him to show her the main control room. Reluctantly, Steve had agreed to her plan. They gave themselves exactly twenty-two minutes before simultaneous switch-pulling. Steve went to the tank while Jaime managed to charm Harris into exactly what she wanted.

But at the crucial moment—the pain! The excruciating, unbearable pain had hit Jaime and she went out of control. Only the incredible power and speed of their bionic legs had enabled Steve and Jaime to pull out of there alive as Harris and his guards emptied their guns in a futile attempt to reach them. They had returned to Oscar, mission incomplete. Jaime had been placed under intense observation, and, shortly afterward, Rudy and Michael had performed the operation that saved her life at the expense of her memory.

But now she remembered all of it. Almost...

Abruptly, she turned her attention back to the present moment. Here was Oscar, getting chalk all over his suit, quietly waiting for her to put it all together. Dear Oscar, so humorless and so kind.

"Tell me about Harris now, Oscar. Why do you think he's a bad guy?"

Oscar brushed his jacket sleeve, and then came over to sit on the edge of Jaime's desk for a serious talk.

"Harris is an extremely shrewd man who skillfully intermixes legitimate business dealings with illegitimate ones. We suspect him of exporting government secrets, but we've never been able to put together any firm proof. And we've lost three agents trying to infiltrate his organization."

"Lost?"

"Permanently."

"Wow."

"Which brings me back to the point. I'm concerned about your safety, Jaime."

Jaime glanced down at the stack of papers. The kids had done very well on their math tests. She was proud of them.

"Apparently Harris is trying to kill you because of your attack on his refinery, so we want you to—"

Jaime had a sudden thought, and she interrupted him. "Wait a minute, Oscar. Why should he want to do that? I messed up on that mission, totally. I didn't do him any harm. And if he really wanted to kill me, wouldn't I be dead by now?''

''But why else would these 'accidents' be happening?'' Oscar said sensibly.

Jaime bit her pencil tip, thinking hard. She looked back at the math tests.

''Do you think maybe he's testing me?'' she said thoughtfully.

''What?''

''He saw me use my bionics at the refinery. Oscar, I'll bet that's it. He's been causing these 'accidents' to find out more about me.''

''Could be,'' Oscar said slowly. ''But why?''

''I dunno . . .'' Her mind was racing. ''Why do you test drive a car? Because you're thinking about buying it,'' she said.

Their eyes met. It made sense.

''Well,'' Oscar said cautiously, ''he's certainly got money enough to make you an attractive offer.''

''Right,'' Jaime answered. ''Look, Oscar, if that *is* what he has in mind, suppose we make it easier for him?''

''What are you talking about?''

''Suppose he thought I was fed up with you and the OSI? It would be the perfect opportunity for me to go over into his camp.''

''Now wait a minute . . .''

''Come on,'' she said, heady with excitement. ''You said yourself how hard it's been for you to get a man into his organization. Maybe a woman would have a better shot.''

''Jaime—''

"Oscar, he might go for it. We can make it look like we've had a fight, and then once I was inside his organization, I could look for some kind of hard criminal evidence to put him away. Oscar, let's try it!"

"No, Jaime. You're not ready for—"

"Listen, I'm more together now than I ever have been. And I owe you. I *want* to help." She felt the blood pulsing through her body and adrenalin charging all the natural and bionic components to a keenness she hadn't felt since her first serve on Court One at Wimbledon. This was what was missing from her life—one of the things—this charge of energy and eagerness to challenge herself to the limits of her abilities.

"All right," Oscar agreed finally, seeing her determination. His finer instincts had long been under pressure because of his job. His special genius was in recruiting people, sizing them up, and converting them to service for the OSI. Jaime was an expensive investment, and she *was* ready. There was no way he could justify holding her back. But this time, she would be on her own—Steve Austin was out of the picture as far as Jaime was concerned, for the foreseeable future, anyway. But looking at her, catching the vibrations of her determination, knowing her intelligence as well as her physical powers, he knew that she was ready. He would be inexcusably derelict in his duty if he put concern for her personal safety before the possible good work she could do. If everything went all right, this time.

"All right," he repeated. "But on one condition, Jaime. Don't make a move until you let me plan this out."

"It's a deal," Jaime said.

She had to laugh at his sour expression. She put her arms around his neck and kissed his cheek.

"Now. Is it possible that those men he sent to watch me are here on the base?" she asked, back to business.

"Very possible," Oscar replied.

"Then brace yourself," she grinned. "I'm about to get mad at you."

Out in the hall, a custodian in army fatigues was leaning on a mop, his bucket of ammoniated solution forgotten as he strained to hear what was being said behind the closed door. He was rewarded, unexpectedly, and stepped back with a start as Jaime's voice rose to a shout.

"No, I've just *had* it with you!"

The custodian had to lean forward again to hear the answer, in a louder but still modulated man's voice.

"But Jaime, you've got to understand—"

"No, I don't."

Dark shadows looming up on the glass window of the classroom door warned the custodian just in time to begin mopping again as Jaime stormed out of the room, with Oscar in close pursuit.

"Jaime, listen to me, budgets are budgets—" She turned to face him angrily. Her voice was shrill. "You know what you can do with your budget. And don't bother to call until you've got a much better offer."

"Jaime—"

But she strode off, leaving him standing alone in the corridor, except for the custodian who was busily mopping the floor.

Oscar sighed loudly and then crossed the hall to a pay phone attached to the wall. From the corner of his eye, he observed that the custodian had moved close enough to him to listen. Oscar dropped his coin and dialed.

"Hello...Mr. Secretary? Oscar Goldman. No, she hasn't come around yet. Still the money problem. Isn't there anything we can do?"

The floor got very clean by the time Oscar hung up in weary resignation, shook his head in defeat, and left the school building.

Chapter Thirteen

Later that afternoon, Jaime vacuumed her apartment—it took a full six minutes, but that was because she lifted all the furniture to get under it. Then she watered the plants, rehung the kitchen curtains, washed some hand laundry, buffed the nails on her left hand (the right hand nails didn't need a thing), and tried to concentrate on a magazine article. When the phone finally rang, she reacted sharply, but forced herself to walk across the room at a normal pace, take a deep breath, and then answer as if she hadn't been waiting for it to ring all that time.

"Hello?"

"Jaime? It's Oscar."

"What do you want?"

"I feel very bad about upsetting you so much."

"Just be glad I didn't get really mad and throw you through a wall," she said with a secret grin.

Oscar chuckled nervously. "Right," he said. "Uh, now, Jaime, I've been on the phone with the Secretary, and we've managed to get a higher Civil Service rating for you, which will mean some more money."

"How much more?"

"It'll be, well...you'll be making pretty close to nineteen thousand a year. And of course you'll get a lot of fringe benefits like—"

She cut him short with a rude noise. "Are you kidding me?"

"What? No...I...uh..."

"Nineteen thousand a year for my services? What do you think I am, some kind of bionic cocktail waitress? Am I supposed to make it on tips?"

"Jaime, will you please be reasonable!"

"I've been reasonable for plenty long enough, Mr. Goldman. Don't call me back until you're ready to talk about some money—and I mean big money!"

She slammed the phone down noisily. She made a face which would have been comical if Oscar could have seen it, a grimace that was part grin and part chagrin. "Sorry, Oscar," she murmured, blowing a kiss at the silent phone.

It worked. On a side road not far from Jaime's apartment, Carlton Harris and two men were huddled over a recording machine inside the small, white, covered van. One of the men was a slim young fellow, serious-faced. The other was the "custodian" of the base school building. Jaime's voice came through clearly on the tape.

"...Don't call me back until you're ready to talk about some money—and I mean big money!"

And then the sound of her phone crashing into its cradle, and the desolate voice of Oscar Goldman against the buzzing on the other end.

"Jaime? Jaime?" He hung up.

"Well, I'd say this is an interesting development," Harris said thoughtfully. "A trifle convenient, perhaps, but interesting."

"Convenient?" the young man queried.

"Still in all, she did seem to be under some kind of mental stress when I first encountered her. Maybe her attitude now is an outgrowth of that." He looked up at the man in army fatigues. "You've done an excellent job, Bailey. Her brake failure this morning was a masterpiece."

"Thank you, Mr. Harris."

"And it certainly showed me once again how special Miss Sommers really is."

"What exactly is so special about her, Dad?" asked the young man.

"You'll see, Donald."

"Dad, can I talk to you for a minute, privately?"

They stepped down from the van, which was hidden from the road in a grove of trees. Harris strode away into the woods a few yards, and his son followed him.

"What's disturbing you, Donald?" Harris asked with a show of impatience. "You've been under a dark cloud ever since you graduated last week."

"What happened to that discussion we had when I started law school?" Donald blurted.

"Which discussion was that?"

"You know which one. You told me that you were planning to concentrate all your efforts on your legitimate business interests, and to drop all the...other ones." Donald's earnest face searched his father's. There was a family resemblance—dark, brooding good looks—but Donald's troubled expression was so far innocent of the cynical, almost sinister cast that

108

marked his father's appearance.

"To a large extent, I've done just that, Donald," Harris said easily. "But you've got to learn something about the definition of 'legitimate.' No business on earth is without some sort of corruption, son. Plato's Utopia does not exist." He put an arm around his son's shoulders and led him to a log where they could sit.

"I understand how you feel. Law school had the same effect on me when I was your age. I came out very much the idealist, like you are, but long experience has taught me that the real world has a sliding scale of values. What may seem corrupt behavior to some is perfectly legitimate behavior to another."

"Hey, Dad, I understand. I'm not that naive. But you make it sound like everyone can be bought."

"Well, I think everyone can be persuaded. But corruption is just a point of view. Now, take Miss Sommers. To her superior, Goldman, she's about to become corrupt. But as far as I'm concerned, she's simply realizing her own worth. A very legitimate growth. You'll see."

"There are laws, Dad."

"She's free to work for whomever she chooses, isn't she? It's free enterprise. Now, come on. I'll call her, and you see for yourself."

They went back to the van, and Harris picked up the telephone. Jaime's phone number was already listed in the notebook he carried.

"Hello?"

"Miss Sommers?"

"Who is this?"

"Carlton Harris." There was a pause. "Do you remember me?"

Jaime's slight hesitation was not faked. "Yes."

"Nice to talk to you again."

The caution in her voice was apparent to both of them, and somehow it eased any apprehensions Harris might have had.

"What do you want?" she asked.

"I want to help you," he said smoothly.

"How?"

"I'm aware of the current negotiation problems you're experiencing with the OSI—"

"I don't know what you're talking about."

"Oh, come, now, Jaime, don't be coy. I'm in a position to make you a very wealthy woman. Now tell me that doesn't interest you."

There was another pause. Then she said, even more cautiously, "It might."

"Of course it does," Harris said, with a significant glance across the van at his son. "But I must move quickly, so if you are interested, meet me in the alley behind the Bank of Ojai in ten minutes. Otherwise we'll forget the whole thing."

"Now, wait—"

"Ten minutes."

He hung up. Jaime stared at the dead phone. "Hello?" But she heard nothing except the drome of the broken connection. And Oscar's voice in her memory.

"Don't make a move until you let me plan this out."

There wasn't time to get to another phone to call him. It would take the full ten minutes to get to the bank if she left this very second. She was up against a clever enemy.

110

She was not unmindful of something else Oscar had told her. As she drove toward Main Street, she remembered the three agents whom Harris had already disposed of, permanently.

Careful, Jaime, she told herself. Plan every serve and be ready for every tricky return. Get to know your opponent. Stay cool.

She arrived at the alley behind the bank exactly ten minutes after the phone conversation. No one else was there. The late afternoon sun was glinting off the tops of the buildings that lined the alley. She looked up and down, and tried to plan an escape from the narrow cul-de-sac, should that suddenly become necessary. But the buildings stood side by side and only the back doors of a few shops faced onto the alley, all of them closed and apparently locked. She waited.

They were parked on a street nearby, out of sight. Harris sat in front of the limousine with the driver, Sayers. Donald was in the back seat, peering out of the one-way windows toward the meeting place.

"She ought to be well in there by now," Sayers said.

"You never did tell me what's so special about her anyway," Donald remarked.

"You're about to see for yourself," his father said. He nodded to Sayers. The driver dropped the car into gear and whipped it around the corner to head down the little alley with a violent thrust of speed.

Donald was thrown back against the calfskin upholstery. He pulled himself forward to demand, "What are you doing!?!"

They all saw Jaime at the same moment. She had been facing the other way, but at the sound of the racing car, she had spun around, and now she stood frozen in the middle of the alley, watching them bear down on her.

"Stop! You'll hit her!" Donald yelled.

His father and Sayers ignored him. All three pairs of eyes were fastened onto the lone, fragile-looking young woman about to be ground to bits under their wheels.

They saw her head spin from one side to the other, hair flying, as she frantically tried to spot an escape route. But the unyielding backs of the buildings faced her on both sides.

"Stop! For God's sake, stop! She can't go anywhere!" Donald screamed.

The car was only a few feet away, covering the graveled ground in split seconds. Jaime saw a fire escape about fifteen feet over her head. She reached her right arm up, and with one adroit movement, she leaped straight into the air and grasped the iron railing with one hand. She hung there as the limousine roared angrily over the spot where she had been standing a split second before.

The car screeched to a halt, throwing cinder against the whitewashed buildings like hailstones. Donald's horrified face was pressed against the rear window. He turned to look at his father, disbelief in his eyes. Harris cocked one eyebrow at his son, as if to say "I told you so." He got out of the car and sauntered over to the fire escape. He looked up at the girl hanging there.

"Well, Miss Sommers, you certainly are very special indeed. And we have a great deal to talk about."

Jaime looked down at him. Her moment of terror had turned to anger, and she didn't disguise it. She bounded down gracefully, landing with a slight bounce on the gravel next to Harris.

She was in it now.

Chapter Fourteen

The blue water caught the last rays of the setting sun. Sailboats were heading home, running with the onshore breeze, skimming and bobbing into the wind as the deep water darkened out on the horizon. Jaime gazed out at the sea, thinking how deceptively calm the surface seemed from this distance.

There was a muted popping sound behind her, and Carlton Harris's voice halted her revery.

"Jaime? Some champagne?"

Aha, the shark was calling her to come and play. Jaime turned from the low terrace wall and accepted the glass he held out to her.

"To your health—and wealth, Jaime."

They sipped at the wine. At that moment, Donald Harris came through the french doors onto the terrace. His father beamed, and poured another glass.

"Ah, Donald. Jaime, did I tell you that Donald just

graduated from Harvard Law School—magna cum laude.''

''Yes, you told me,'' she said. She raised her champagne with a slight motion in Donald's direction.

''I'm very proud of my boy,'' Harris went on. ''Someday, all this will be his.'' His gesture included not only the mountaintop villa and terraced grounds, but the Pacific Ocean as well.

''Listen, Carlton,'' Jaime said, ''did you keep that armed guard outside my room all night just so I could get to know your son today, or are we going to talk money?''

Donald stared at her, obviously thinking that she was an exceptionally disagreeable character. Any attraction he had felt for her magnificent good looks was certainly dissipated now.

''Money, yes,'' Carlton Harris said, unperturbed.

He went over to the portable television monitor and switched it on. In an instant, the tape of Sayers's ''accident'' flashed on the screen. They watched as the car passed Jaime on the road, collided at the intersection, and spun off into the gulley; and they watched Jaime's remarkable rescue.

''You're a regular Allen Funt, aren't you?'' she sneered.

''And you're a fascinating blend of beauty and truly remarkable strength. How are you able to do things like that?''

Jaime set the champagne glass down on the table. She sat back in her chair and told him. ''I was in a skydiving accident. I lost both legs and an arm. So I let Goldman make me a guinea pig, to test their bionic theories.''

"Is it just your legs and your arm?" Harris wanted to know.

Jaime lied without hesitation. "Yes."

"Exactly how strong are you?" Harris asked.

Jaime looked around the terrace. A heavy wrought iron planter stood near her chair. Without getting up, she reached out her right hand, grasped the stand casually, and bent it almost double. The plant came clattering to the tile floor.

"Strong enough," she said.

Harris and his son stared at her, stunned.

The older man recovered his composure at once. "Fascinating," he said. "It makes me want to overlook the fact that you so conveniently have decided to join forces with me."

Jaime knew she was in control of the situation now. "Let's get something straight, Mr. Harris. I haven't decided anything. And you are just my first offer." She reached for the glass of champagne and, holding it at arm's length, poured the liquid onto the imported Greek tiles. She set the glass down again, stood up and said calmly, "I'm ready to go home now."

"Now don't misunderstand, Jaime," Carlton said, a tinge of anxiety betraying him. "I am anxious to have you join my organization—"

"Really? I haven't heard an offer yet."

Harris, recovering his sleek poise, leaned over to refill her glass. "True," he said. "How would you like to make one million dollars in the next twenty-four hours?"

Donald gasped audibly, then he shrugged and shook his head in obvious admiration for his father's tactics. Jaime quickly stifled her own startled gasp.

"Well, uh, that *is* an offer," she managed to say.

Donald was watching her closely, still not completely convinced that this tanned, tawny-haired, lovely young woman was up for sale to the highest bidder.

"It also sounds like whatever I've got to do isn't quite legal," she added.

Harris glanced at his son, who was waiting for the answer, too.

"Well," Harris said, "there are various definitions of legal . . ."

"What do I have to do? ' Jaime asked bluntly.

"There are several items that I wish to acquire from some of my industrial competitors," Harris said.

"And you want me to steal those things for you."

"To put it coldly, yes. Now, we have an opportunity to acquire the first item by attending a formal party this evening."

"A formal party?" Jaime echoed. She looked down at herself, still dressed in the polished cotton jumpsuit she had worn since the day before. It was attractive, but hardly suitable for a formal party.

"But I haven't a thing to wear," she said. "I'll have to go out for a while to get some clothes. I mean, I couldn't go in this."

"But that's quite attractive, particularly on you," Harris said, and for a flash-second Jaime could understand why he had the reputation of being a ladies' man—or lady-killer, as Steve had reminded her. Harris continued, "There is, however, no need to leave my little compound here. I think we can find some clothes for you, assuming we have a deal. Do we?"

Their eyes met. Each tried to read the other, and

117

each tried to hide something from the other. "Yes," Jaime said finally.

"Excellent!" Harris smiled and rose from his chair. "Follow me," he said, and went inside the house.

Jaime got up to follow him. Passing the thoughtful Donald, she grinned at him. "Does your father always come on like this?" she asked.

Donald's answer was partly a nod and partly a shrug. His smile was hard to read, but seemed to indicate a certain attempt at cynicism. Jaime wondered about Donald. How much part did he have in his father's dealings? Were there two enemies to watch out for here? She gave him her brightest smile and then walked on past him into the house.

Harris led her across the enormous glass-walled living room through a wide passageway where lush plants and fresh-cut flowers made the house seem part of the mountain itself. They entered the bedroom wing, and she followed him into a luxurious room lined with mirrored doors. He opened them, one after another, until one entire wall was revealed as a series of closets holding dozens of beautiful dresses, coats, shoes, blouses, pantsuits, and outfits of all descriptions.

Jaime was impressed. The clothes were obviously expensive, and enough to dress a dozen stylish women. She touched a bright print silk and a soft cashmere. "They're beautiful," she said sincerely.

"They're only the beginning, my dear," Harris said. He kissed her hand. Jaime had all she could do not to pull it away, but she smiled. Then, as he moved closer for what threatened to be a frontal assault, Jaime gracefully stepped aside.

"Ummm," she parried, "if we're going to a party, it's going to take me a while to get dressed."

"Fine," Harris agreed, unruffled. "Needless to say, I'm delighted to have you with us." He seemed to be implying that there would be plenty of time for what he had in mind.

"And I'm delighted to be here," she said.

Confident, Harris left the room, and Jaime's smile faded. "You snake," she whispered under her breath.

She looked around the room, and moved toward the ivory telephone. It was probably bugged, but she decided to try anyway. Yes, there it was, the little clicking in her bionic ear. She set the phone back down. There was no way to reach Oscar now.

Oscar was talking on his own phone, miles away.

"She hasn't tried to call you either?" he was saying.

"No," Helen's worried voice answered. "And apparently she didn't come home at all last night. I checked her apartment. What does it mean, Oscar?"

"She's doing a little work for me, that's all, Helen. But she was supposed to contact me first." There was a pause, and then Oscar added, "All we can do now is wait."

"What kind of work, Oscar? Can you tell us?"

"Some security work. Nothing too serious. Now, I'm going to station one of my men at her place and another one with you at the house. Twenty-four hours a day, just in case she tries to get a message through."

"If you're going to do that," Helen said slowly, "then it must be serious, Oscar. You are worried about her, aren't you?"

"Oh, not really," Oscar bluffed. "She'll be fine."

"You hope," Helen finished for him, and she sighed.

"I'll talk to you later and let you know if we hear anything at all," Oscar promised, and Helen had to be content with that.

Chapter Fifteen

Jaime chose a long gown that fit her as if it had been made for her—as if someone had been studying her so carefully that they had every millimeter of her measurements. But her delight in the shimmering soft silk gown overpowered her useless speculations. It was a stunner. A jewel box lying on top of the dressing table had proved to be filled with magnificent necklaces and earrings and brooches. She selected a diamond choker and long teardrop earrings that complemented the crystal insets handsewn into the low-cut bodice of the sapphire blue dress. Her tan skin and naturally glowing eyes needed no makeup—a touch of lipstick and she was ready. Her hair was piled in soft tendrils. She was just brushing the last lock in place when there was a knock on her door.

"Who is it?" she called.

"Donald Harris. Are you decent?"

"Almost. Come on in," she said.

Donald looked quite handsome in his black tie. He smiled pleasantly at her and then glanced around at the extravagant array of clothes strewn over the bed and chairs. Jaime was amused at his expression.

"It was hard to decide what to wear," she said solemnly, looking at his reflection in the long dressing table mirror. "You know, I've had my differences with your father, but it's sure tough not to like someone who gives you such terrific things."

"Yeah. Dad always tries to stack the deck in his favor," Donald said.

"What's wrong with that?"

Donald hesitated. "Nothing, I guess," he said finally.

Jaime rose from the vanity bench and stood before him. "You like?" she said.

Donald was truly captivated. She saw the approval in his eyes. "Very much," he said.

"Hook me up, will you?" She turned her back to him. She had managed the zipper, but the miniscule hook at the nape of her neck had escaped her. She knew what she was doing, she hoped—enlisting him on her side, if it were possible.

"You're very beautiful," Donald said as he fumbled with the clasp.

"I'm glad to see you can talk," she said.

"You're not hard to talk to."

"Out there on the terrace, your father didn't give you a chance."

"You could say he's kind of dominant," Donald agreed. "But he means well. There, it's closed." He stepped away and Jaime turned to face him.

"Does he? Mean well, I mean?"

"I think so," Donald said seriously. "He's really a pretty nice man. Do you know he gives all kinds of money to charities?''

Jaime looked down at the open jewel box. Maybe she would hang on a bracelet, too, as long as they were there. Or would it be too much? Not forgetting her role, she picked it up. ''Frankly,'' she said, ''I don't care what kind of man he is, as long as he supplies things like these.''

Donald's hand reached out to touch an ermine wrap that was flung over the back of a chair. ''Do you really need it, though?'' he asked.

''What do you mean?''

''Well, you were a successful tennis pro. You must have made a comfortable income, and now with your teaching . . .''

Jaime laughed. ''There's comfortable and . . .'' she flicked her finger against the sparkling earrings that hung cold against her neck, ''. . . comfortable,'' she said. ''You understand?''

''Only too well,'' Donald replied.

He's got his doubts, Jaime thought to herself. How far do they extend?

She tested him. ''Sounds to me like your father's actions don't always please you,'' she said tentatively.

''I guess you just don't seem like the kind of person who'd let yourself be bought so easily,'' he said.

Oh-oh, was he testing her now? She'd better play it really tough and hard, not take any chances. She threw herself into the role with as much passion as she could simulate.

''Well, all I know is that I'm a *very* special person,'' she said. ''And if I can work for someone who really appreciates my abilities and is willing to reward me royally, why should I turn down that kind of opportunity?''

''I guess you shouldn't, if that's where your head is,'' Donald replied.

''Where's *your* head?'' she asked, facing him squarely.

They tried to size each other up. Come on, Donald, she thought to herself, make a stand, one way or another. But all he said was, ''Come on, my father will be waiting.''

He reached into the coat closet for a dark black mink and held it for her to slip into. It draped weightlessly down to the floor in soft, warm folds. Jaime managed to suppress her aversion to wearing animal skins, and they left the room together.

Carlton Harris was waiting for them in the living room. He saluted her appearance with deeply appreciative eyes.

''Jaime, you look marvelous,'' he exclaimed.

''Thanks,'' she said. ''I guess now I'll have to start earning the clothes, huh? Not to mention the diamonds?''

They stepped out into the cool evening, and Jaime took a deep breath of the tangy ocean air before getting into the limousine. She sat in the back between them.

''Well, let me explain what has to be done,'' Harris said. ''We're on our way to the estate of Charles Butler, an industrial designer. He is a friend and a competitor. His design laboratory is in his home, and in his safe is a packet of designs for something called Project Rebound.''

''And you want that packet,'' Jaime said.

''*We* want that packet,'' he corrected her. He ran his hand over the sleeve of the black mink coat. ''Remember," he pointed out, "we're all in this together now."

Jaime couldn't resist a sidelong smile at Donald. He sat staring straight ahead. She wondered about him. Clearly, he hadn't made up his mind. Which way would he jump when the chips started flying? It looked like she wouldn't know until it happened.

The Butler mansion sat high on another mountain-top farther up the beach. No other houses could be seen as they stepped out of the car. Only the stars, and the slowly rising moon reflecting on the vast deserted ocean below them. From the house, sounds of an orchestra could be heard, behind the clink of glasses and the low chatter of a large group of people.

Their host met them just inside the door and showed his delight clearly on his round, benign face.

"Jaime Sommers!" he exclaimed. He handed her a glass of champagne from a tray being passed by a waiter. "I'm really tickled to have you here, Jaime. I could use some advice on my backhand."

Charles Butler was balding, and fiftyish, with a warm friendly smile. He spoke with a slight midwestern twang, and his admiration for Jaime was obvious.

"You play tennis?" Jaime asked him.

"Well, I play at it and figure I've done all right if I don't injure myself," the genial Butler joked.

Jaime laughed. "I'm sure it's not that bad. You know, everybody has trouble with the backhand. It was the weakest part of my game."

"Honey," Butler breathed fervently at her, "I saw you play and I know better."

"She was quite a player, wasn't she?" Carlton Harris put in.

"Yup," Butler nodded. "And you know what amazes me?"

"What?" Jaime asked.

"Just look at this arm," Butler said. He lifted Jaime's right hand and held her arm up for everyone to see. "It's so hard to imagine that something so delicate and feminine could have so much strength," he marveled.

Harris tried to catch Jaime's eye for a secret smile between them, but she avoided looking at him and played it with a completely straight face. "Well," she said pleasantly, "there's a little more there than meets the eye."

Butler stared at her hungrily. He was like a big teddy bear, in need of affection but harmless, she decided. "Lemme tell ya," he said, breathing recycled champagne fumes in her face, "what does meet the eye is mighty pleasing."

Jaime blushed and looked over at Carlton Harris. He got her into this, maybe he'd like to get her out, too.

"Charlie," Harris said smoothly, "isn't that Dee Parkinson over there?"

"Ah! He showed up after all! 'Scuse me, Jaime." He relinquished his grip on her arm and walked off.

"Well, my dear, you are a hit," Harris whispered to her.

"That's what you're paying me for, isn't it?" she replied tartly.

"No. What I'm paying you for is to get that packet."

Jaime swallowed hard. "Now?"

"Yes. His design lab is three doors down that hallway, on the left. The vault is inside.''

'She handed him her untouched champagne glass and walked in the direction he indicated. With the other guests milling about between them, neither Carlton nor Jaime noticed Donald Harris following her out of the room.

The hallway was empty, and she had no trouble finding the door marked "Design Laboratory—No Admittance." She gripped the heavy knob with her right hand, twisted it with one thrust of her bionic power, and the lock gave way like tinfoil. She entered the room and closed the door behind her.

The room was dark, except for the moonlight outlining the equipment shelves, drafting tables, and the large desk. The safe was against the far wall, behind the desk.

Jaime went to it and knelt down to pull at the handle. The heavy steel lock twisted into a corkscrew and then broke under her tremendous strength. Quickly, she dug her fingernails into the metal and pulled open the solid steel door.

She was too absorbed to notice the door to the lab opening a crack behind her. Donald Harris put his eye to the opening and watched her silently.

Jaime peeled the metal from the door of the safe and reached inside. She found the packet, and held it up to the ray of moonlight so she could read the large red label that covered it.

"PROJECT REBOUND. PROPERTY OF U.S. GOVERNMENT. TOP SECRET."

She frowned. Then she leaned over to the desk and took up a pen and paper. With bionic speed, she wrote a note. It said, "Contact Goldman, OSI."

Jaime knelt to the safe once more, and placed her note inside. Then she stood up, slid the packet under the folds of her mink coat, and moved to the door that opened onto a terrace. She let herself out, not making a sound, and closed the door behind her.

The room was quiet. Donald Harris slipped inside. He went to the safe and reached through the jagged opening. He pulled out Jaime's note and read it.

After a long moment, Donald stood up. He put Jaime's note in his pocket. Then he went to rejoin his father.

Chapter Sixteen

"You were magnificent, Jaime," Harris said. He poured brandy into two Baccarat glasses and handed her one. He raised his glass in a toast to her, and then toward the "Project Rebound" packet which lay prominently on the silver tray between them. He took a slow, satisfied sip of the mellow brandy.

"I'm glad you're pleased," she said.

"Very much so. We're going to make millions together. Now—the second item must also be collected tonight."

"You really don't waste any time, do you?"

"We can't afford to. I'm acquiring these items for some buyers who must take delivery in the morning. Now, for this next gambit you'll need some special clothing and a certain look. There's a sketch along with your clothes laid out up in your bedroom."

Jaime set her untouched brandy back on the tray and got up from the deep leather couch. Carlton Harris leaned forward to put his hand over hers. "But don't go just yet. Give me another few minutes to admire you," he said.

"Oh, Carlton..." This might start getting tricky. She didn't want to offend him until she was positive that Oscar was in the picture. But she had to play along for a while—and although Harris was an attractive man, he was certainly nowhere near her type.

"I'm really quite drawn to you," he was saying. "Certainly you can sense that. I'm sure that's part of the reason I've let myself trust you."

He was just putting his hands on her bare shoulders when the door to the study opened. Donald stood there, looking like he might back out again when he saw them standing so close together. But he overcame a momentary embarrassment, and his chin jutted forward in a gesture of determination. "Dad, I need to talk to you for a moment. Alone."

"Of course, Donald," Carlton said. "Jaime was just going up to change. Do hurry, my dear," he said in a low voice both sensuous and businesslike.

"I'll be down soon," she said. She stopped at the doorway and peered at Donald. "Hey," she said, "you okay?"

Donald had something on his mind. He looked even more troubled than he had earlier in the evening. But he looked at her evenly and said, "I'm fine."

"Okay," Jaime said cheerfully. She went on past him out of the study. Donald closed the door.

She stayed right there. She didn't even have to strain to hear their low voices; in fact, her bionic ear picked up their movements as well, despite the thick walls of the paneled study.

She heard someone rustling a piece of paper, but the sound was muffled, as though nervous fingers were

129

folding and refolding it deep inside a coat pocket. And then she heard Carlton Harris say, ''Now, then, Donald, what's the trouble?''

''It's . . . it's about . . . uh . . . ''

''Quit fumfering, Donald. Fix yourself a brandy, or something.''

''Yes, I think I will.''

She heard Donald cross the room, but not the expected sound of the bottle lifted or liquid being poured. Instead, there was another subtle sound of papers being handled.

Donald's voice sharpened as he read aloud, ''Property of the U.S. Government . . . Top Secret. Is this what Jaime stole tonight?''

''That's right.''

''But you told me that all you were doing was just a little intermural business-industrial skirmishing.''

''And that's basically all I *am* doing,'' was Harris's calm reply. ''Now just relax.''

''But Dad, what are you involved in? I mean . . . the government . . . ''

''Donald, Donald, my boy, you really must learn to put yourself above business interests. Even above government interests. I've told you—it's all corrupt, to one degree or another.''

''But top-secret material . . . ''

''Donald.'' Jaime heard the brandy bottle being lifted from the tray, now, and two glasses being poured out. ''Everybody steals from everybody,'' Harris went on in a quiet voice. ''Everybody does it. It's nothing new. It was done before you were born. It was done before I was born. And the results are bountiful.''

"But that doesn't make it right, Dad."

"It depends on your point of view, Donald. Now, take this latest transaction. It simply involves our collecting plans and a few key components for a new sonar device. It happens to be classified right now, which is why it is so valuable. The Navy is developing it for its nuclear submarines."

Jaime's eyes opened wide as she took this in. She desperately wished she could get to a phone, but right now her job was to listen for all she was worth. Carlton Harris was sounding quite proud of himself as he explained his clever dealings to his son and heir.

"Why, one of my companies even has a contract to supply one of the components. That's how I first became aware of Project Rebound and its value. Now, I've got some very powerful foreign buyers who'll be here to take delivery at eight o'clock in the morning. To them, what we're doing is very 'right.' " Harris sounded not only proud, but downright delighted with himself. "As you grow a little older and wiser, you'll gain a broader perspective about these things," he went on. "And now, then . . . did you want to see me about something?"

There was no response for a long moment, and Jaime had to lean toward the door to catch Donald's next words.

"It . . . it was about Jaime," he said finally.

She caught her breath and waited.

"Well?" Harris said, impatiently.

"I . . . I'll talk to you later," Donald answered. "I have to find out something first."

"So it wasn't so important after all?"

Not to you, buddy, but it sure is to me, Jaime was

thinking. She wondered and knew she had to find out what was on Donald's mind before his father did . . . whatever it was.

"All right. We'd better get going. We have to move quickly now. I don't want to disappoint my buyers. I've got to see if Jaime is ready yet."

By the time he had set his brandy down and crossed the room to the door, Jaime had taken off in a bionic run down the thickly carpeted hall, and thrust herself in one leap to the landing above the stairs. She ducked into her room and was out of the long gown in two seconds flat.

With no time to wonder about the costume which was laid out on her bed, she slipped into the dark skirt and white lab jacket. She pulled her hair back to fit the image which clearly went with the tortoise-shell glasses and sensible shoes. In two minutes, she was emerging from her bedroom to find Harris just arriving at her door with his hand raised to knock.

"Fine," he said, approvingly. "Now, come on, I'll tell you about it on the way to the car."

She listened carefully to his instructions. Outside, they walked around to the back of the lower terrace that led to the rear of the driveway. A small white covered van was there. On its panel, a sign read "Perry Scientific, Inc."

"Once you've gotten into the complex," Harris was saying, "what you're after is an electronic component, the LV13 Sonic Modulator. It should be in the room which I described. Any questions?"

"No," Jaime answered.

"Okay. Good luck," he said, and opened the door of the van for her. She climbed into the passenger seat and the driver started up immediately. Jaime looked over at him as they pulled out of the circular driveway.

"Why, Donald!"

"That's right. You don't mind if I go along with you?"

In profile, Donald showed a strong chin line, and if it hadn't been for a single lock of hair which tumbled across his forehead, he might have looked quite severe, even fierce. Jaime was puzzled. Why was Donald along? To spy on her—or to trap her? Either way, it was going to make things difficult.

"Well, do you mind?" he repeated.

"Oh, uh . . . no, I guess not," she said.

"I mean, you don't have anything to hide, do you?"

"Of course not," she answered quickly. But she'd have to be very, very careful. Whose side was Donald on, anyway? The only smart thing was to figure that he was working for Daddy all the way. Then why hadn't he told Carlton whatever it was he "knew" about her? And what did he know, anyway? What was it he had told his father he was going to "find out"?

Donald pulled the wheel around to turn in at the entrance gate of a large complex of low buildings surrounded by a high wall. The guard stepped over to the van, and Donald showed an identity card. The guard looked at it and then handed it back and waved them through the gate.

In answer to Jaime's raised eyebrow, Donald showed her the card. "My father owns a very good engraving plant, too," he said.

He steered the little truck down a center street and stopped in front of a small white building. Jaime opened her door. "Okay," she said, "you wait here. I can probably do better in there by myself."

"Yes, I'm sure you can," Donald said.

She grinned at him, but he didn't smile back. She got out of the van, keenly aware of his eyes on her back as she slipped inside the building.

In the hall, she passed a technician dressed in a lab smock identical to her own. They nodded at each other and she kept right on walking until she reached a door marked "Component Storage—Security Area." The door was bolted with a heavy padlock. Jaime stopped, and looked up and down the hall. It was empty.

She twisted the padlock with one motion, and pushed the heavy door open. She stepped inside the dark room. As the door swung shut behind her, an automatic light went on, revealing a windowless storage room, with wooden crates piled neatly in rows, labeled and classified by contents. A large wire cage enclosed some boxes in a corner of the room. Jaime moved toward it. Through the heavy wire mesh she could read the labels on the boxes: "LV13." This was it.

Jaime used her bionic fingernails to cut through the heavy mesh, and in a moment she had reached inside the security cage to retrieve the unit. She turned to a table nearby and set the component down. She picked up a pen from the neat row on the table, and began to scrawl a message on the memo pad next to the telephone. At bionic speed, her fingers flew across the page: Contact Goldman, OSI—target is Navy Sonar Unit—sale due in ten hours—will advise location . . .

"Leaving another note?"

Jaime gasped. Donald Harris was pointing a pistol at her. It was equipped with a silencer, and now there

134

was no doubt about whose side he was on. He reached into his pocket and took out a crumpled piece of paper. He showed it to her across the long evil nose of the gun. It was her first note, left in Butler's safe, but slated never to be seen by Butler. Or Oscar.

"Now pick up that note," Donald said sharply, "and the component. That's right. Now, let's go. We have some problems to discuss."

Chapter Seventeen

While Jaime was being led from the high-security lab at gunpoint, Oscar Goldman was standing in Charles Butler's study, staring at the safe with its rather obvious clue that she had been there.

"When did you discover the theft?" he asked Butler.

"About two hours after the last guest left my party," Butler said. "I can't figure it out. How could somebody get into it like that without using dynamite or something?"

"It is pretty remarkable, isn't it?" Oscar agreed.

"You know, the more I look at it, the more it looks like somebody just pulled it apart. But that's impossible!"

"Of course it is," Oscar nodded solemnly. "Charles, did you keep a guest book tonight?"

"Sure thing. I've got it right over here." Butler reached for the book and handed it to Oscar.

He scanned the list of signatures and found exactly what he had expected: "Carlton Harris, Donald Harris, and Jaime Sommers," all signed in the same expansive hand. Oscar's expression showed no giveaway clue, however, and he continued to run his eye down the list of names until the end. He handed the book back to Butler with a nod.

"I really feel terrible about this, Oscar. I know you and the Secretary trusted me to keep my copies of the sonar designs safe." Distress had turned Butler's amiable features into a puckered frown characteristic of a classic anxiety syndrome. His skin was patchy-red, and sweat stood on his forehead in large droplets.

"It's still possible that they might be safe, Charles. I know who's behind the theft."

"You do? Can you tell me?" Relief swept Butler's face. He wiped his temples with a linen handkerchief.

Oscar smiled. "Hey, you know I've got to keep my trade secrets. But I've got one of my agents right on top of it, working inside the thief's organization."

"Well, I sure am glad to hear that!"

"The only real concern I have is not being able to communicate with my agent," Oscar admitted.

"Can I help?"

Oscar shook his head. "I'm afraid this agent is going to have to do it alone. All we can do right now is stand by and wait. And hope," he added.

Oscar had one clue, anyway. Now he knew part of what Carlton Harris was after. He headed back to his office at the OSI to start analyzing all the possible uses of the Project Rebound data which had been stolen from Butler and spent the rest of the night waiting for a phone call. It was a long, sleepless, futile night.

"You know, if you shoot me, I'm not going to be able to drive very well."

137

"Pull off to the side up here," Donald answered crisply. He was holding the gun close to her side.

"Now *that* worries me," Jaime said. She glanced at his stern frowning face.

"Pull over, Jaime," he repeated.

She steered the van to the side of the road. It was pitch-dark and deserted.

"Turn off the engine," Donald ordered.

She did. The night was eerily silent, except for the lonely echoing hoot of an owl now and then.

"You're a spy, aren't you?" Donald said quietly. "Working undercover for the OSI?"

Jaime looked at him and then down at the gun which was grazing her ribs. She sighed.

"When you're right, you're right," she said.

"You know, in a way, I'm glad," Donald said.

"What?" She really didn't understand that one.

"I guess I really didn't want to believe that you'd sell out so easily," he explained.

"Why?"

"I don't know. I guess...I like you, Jaime." But she still felt the cold steel of the gun nudging her through the starched white smock. She shivered.

"Is that why you didn't show my first note to your father? Or *did* you show it to him?"

"No, I didn't. I was going to, and then I realized that Project Rebound is top-secret government material."

"That's right," Jaime said. "Now that you know both sides, what are you going to do?"

Donald's hand toyed with the silencer, his fingers running nervously up and down the glinting length of it as he talked. "Jaime," he said, "I want you to under-

138

stand something. I love my father. I feel a responsibility to protect him. And more than that, I really respect his abilities . . .''

An ardent feeling of pride came into his voice.

''I mean, you should see him walk into a business meeting and take command. He's really special. And he can be warm and compassionate, too. Look, I know nobody's perfect. I know he's slipped off the straight and narrow once in a while—''

''You can say that again,'' Jaime ventured.

''All right. I know all that, but I also know how important Project Rebound is.''

''What are you getting at, Donald?''

He stared at her across the quiet dark. This time, it seemed that their eyes really were trying to find the truth about each other. Jaime felt a surge of concern for Donald's mixed loyalties, and with it a moment's hope that maybe—maybe—she could get through to him. ''I'd like to make a deal,'' he said finally.

''What kind of a deal?''

''I'll return the Project Rebound material in exchange for my father's freedom.''

''I couldn't do that even if I wanted to, Donald,'' Jaime said with a sigh. ''Your father's done a lot worse than just 'slip off the straight and narrow once in a while.' ''

Donald pulled back. The gun stayed in her ribs. ''What are you talking about?''

Quietly, Jaime said, ''Your father has been responsible for the deaths of three OSI agents.''

''I . . I don't believe you.''

''It's true. He even took a shot at me once.''

Donald's eyes flashed and his voice turned angry.

"No," he said. "He wouldn't do something like that. He couldn't. I don't believe you."

"Donald, did you ever think that you could do something like pointing a gun at someone? Is that what you went to law school for?"

They both looked down at the gun. Was she imagining it, or was his hand less steady than before?

"It happens, Donald," she said. "Corruption starts small, but it gets out of hand pretty quickly."

He was still staring down at the gun. After a long moment, he lowered it. He held it, barrel down, with both hands gripping it tightly.

"I still can't believe that he ... how do I know that you're telling me the truth?"

"I'm sorry, Donald, but it *is* true. There's probably some kind of proof hidden away somewhere, and that's what I was doing—trying to find that proof. Now I've got to prevent his sale of the sonar unit as well." She tried to see his reaction, but his face was downcast and the shadows hid him. "Are you going to expose me, Donald?" she asked.

It was an interminable time before he answered. He shook his head a couple of times, trying to clear his thinking.

"If ... if what you say about him is true ..."

"Yes?"

"If it *is* true, and if I can prove it to myself, then I ... I couldn't stand in your way," he said.

Jaime's sympathies went out to him, to his turmoil and pain. She reached across the pistol to touch his hand.

Chapter Eighteen

He picked up the phone before the first ring had stopped.

"Carlton Harris speaking."

"Carlton? This is Charlie Butler."

"Yes, Charles?"

"Sorry to call you so late, but I had a little trouble here tonight, and I thought I ought to let you know about it. Sort of one government contractor to another."

"What's the problem?"

"Well, I'm calling all my friends who have companies involved with Project Rebound. Someone broke in here tonight and stole the designs for the heart of the sonar unit."

"My God, Charlie, that's terrible!"

"Yes...right out from under my nose. I thought you might want to tighten up your own security a little."

"I'll see to it right away. Are there any leads?"

Outside his study window, Harris saw the white van

pulling into the driveway. He tried to keep the satisfaction from creeping into his voice as he continued the conversation.

"Well, my friend Oscar Goldman from the OSI is into it," Butler went on.

"Suddenly Harris was listening very carefully. "Goldman?" he repeated. "Glad to hear that."

"I knew you would be. He's really on top of who stole it. Says he's got one of his agents working on the inside."

Harris, who had been idly admiring Jaime's long tan legs as she stepped down from the van outside his window, suddenly felt his blood turn to ice water. "He does?" he asked with studied calm. His eyes narrowed as they followed Jaime's movements.

"Yep. The OSI is a pretty sharp organization," Butler was saying.

Harris didn't answer him. His attention was on the two young people coming toward him. Especially on the girl. The agent.

"Carlton? Are you there?" the voice on the phone queried.

"Yes, Charlie. Just thinking over what you said. Thanks very much for calling. I'm very glad to have that information."

He hung up the telephone and arranged his mouth in a welcoming smile.

When Jaime and Donald came into the study with the stolen component, Carlton Harris was effusive in his praise, commending them both for a job well done. Then he suggested that they should all retire, since the plan called for a very early job in the morning.

It was barely dawn when she was awakened by a

knock on her door. She called out that she was awake, and forced herself into a brisk cold shower. A few minutes later, she was dressed in a tailored pantsuit of mulberry-colored denim, with espadrilles to match.

"Do you always get up this early on Sunday morning?" she murmured as she got into the limousine with Harris.

"When there's work to be finished," he swid.

"Is this the last item we have to 'acquire'?"

"Yes, and it's going to require all your bionic skills to get it," he said. "You'll have to be sort of a bionic cat burglar."

"What do I do?"

"You're going to infiltrate this electronics firm, Electrodyne, Inc. It's a top security building." He pulled out a diagram from his pocket, and spread it open for her to see. "Your route is over this electrified fence and across open ground to this building. You have to leap up to this second-story window and get through it. Then you'll be in a room with a large vault. Once you get inside the vault, you should find a padded yellow envelope containing a printed circuit."

"That's it?"

"Correct."

"Okay," Jaime said. As he was folding the diagram and putting it back into his pocket, she glanced out of the car window and said casually, "I didn't see Donald this morning. Did you?"

Harris glanced at her. "No. Why?"

"No reason, just curious."

"You should always be careful about curiosity," Harris said. "Remember what it did to the cat."

Did she detect a somewhat less than genial warning

behind that remark?... He had seemed a bit chillier toward her this morning, but it was probably just the tension of coming close to his goal. Still, Jaime was sensitive to the vibrations in the air and unexpectedly found herself with a full-blown case of the jitters.

They said nothing more until Sayers pulled the car up on a deserted side street, next to a high wire fence. Jaime opened the door of the limousine and started to get out.

"Wait five minutes and then make your move," Harris said.

"Right." She smiled at him. "Wish me luck?"

"Yes. You'll need it," he said shortly. He pulled the door shut and the car drove off. Jaime stood on the sidewalk and watched it turn the corner.

The sign under which she waited said "This Fence Electrified—Do Not Touch!" But the sign under which the limousine turned, just around the corner from where she waited, read, "Electrodyne, Inc. A Carlton Harris Industry."

The limousine pulled up at the main office building, and Harris stepped out. He leaned toward the driver's window. "Go tell your guests I'll be joining them in a moment."

"Yes, sir," Sayers said and pulled the car around to the reception area.

Harris went inside. The Sunday quiet permeated the plant, and he was taken aback to find the door of his private office slightly ajar. He entered cautiously, one hand on a bulge in his pocket.

Donald was seated behind his father's desk. Papers and file folders were strewn across the top. He looked up when his father entered. Donald's eyes were weary

144

and angry.

"Good morning, Dad."

"Well, it looks like you've been busy," Harris said. He strode toward the desk. "Are you finally getting interested in my business affairs?"

"You've lied to me," Donald said.

"What are you talking about?"

Donald held up a fistful of papers. "I'm talking about this. I'm talking about what I found in your safe last night."

Harris glanced at the open safe behind his desk. "You shouldn't have gone in there, Donald," he said in a low, ominous tone.

"But I have."

"That is my private file."

"I'm sure it is, because it certainly spells out how corrupt your business dealings are. Corrupt and violent."

"Donald, put that material back."

"That wouldn't make it go away, Dad. Those letters clearly implicate you in the deaths of three men."

"Put them back, Donald."

"Is that all you can say? Don't you feel any remorse? Don't you feel anything? What kind of a man are you?"

Harris was getting angry. His hand went involuntarily to the pocket where he kept his small automatic. But this was his son, and he knew he couldn't solve this problem the easy way.

"Now you climb down off your high horse and remember that I'm your father. How dare you set yourself up as my judge and jury?"

"Dad, you had three people *killed!*"

"The world can be a difficult place, Donald. It's survival of the fittest. It always has been. You'll learn to realize that when—"

"I don't want to learn any more from you! Not from you!"

Harris was fighting to control himself. His fists clenched, but he kept his voice level.

"Donald, I'm very proud of you, and I want very much to have you with me. But if you have no desire to share in my business, then you may leave. I think you'd be very foolish to do that. I'm about to make the biggest sale of my career. I'm about to show my foreign buyers something that's worth fifty times more than the Project Rebound sonar unit." As he spoke, he moved slowly backward toward the door of the office. When he reached it, he paused and said, "I would like to think I have you with me, son. Wealth and power are the keys to all things, Donald. Think twice before you throw those keys away."

He went out. Donald let the fistful of papers fall to the desk, and he buried his face in his trembling hands.

The five minutes were up. Jaime took visual gauge of the height of the fence and then leaped over it, clearing the wires at the top by an easy two feet. She landed on the other side with a graceful bounce, and ran at top speed across the ground toward the building she had been shown on the diagram.

Inside that building, Carlton Harris and his two foreign friends watched her coming toward them on a television monitor.

"I know how interested you are in the sonar unit," Harris was saying with a smile, "but I thought Miss Sommers would be far more interesting to you."

The men watched in fascination as Jaime ran effortlessly, hair flying and lovely features showing no effort, at about thirty miles an hour.

"Once you've seen all she can do," Harris went on smoothly, "I'm sure that you'll be more than anxious to pay handsomely for her. And, gentlemen, she is for sale."

Both of the guests nodded, not taking their eyes from the screen.

Chapter Nineteen

Jaime reached the building and came to a halt. She looked up at the second-story window and, without hesitating, leaped easily toward it. Her right hand grasped the ledge, and she vaulted through to land gracefully on her feet inside.

The closed-circuit viewers saw her glance around the room and then spot a telephone. She tossed her long hair back with one hand and reached for the phone. They saw her listen for a second and then replace the receiver. Then she picked up a flow pen from a desk and began to write across the formica top in large letters. Her fingers flew so swiftly that the hidden camera had to zoom in to catch the motion. In less than a second, she had scribbled a message: CONTACT GOLDMAN, OSI—URGENT! GO TO HARRIS ESTATE IMMEDIATELY!

Jaime turned so quickly she was a blur on the screen, and now the camera moved to allow its private viewers an extraordinary sight. At the huge wall vault, the slim young woman was grasping the lock mechanism with one hand. The heavy metal crumpled under her fingers until the locking device ruptured and she peeled it away.

She opened the vault door and entered the dark interior. Suddenly a bright light flashed on, blinding her for an instant.

"Welcome, Jaime."

She was too startled to speak. She blinked against the harsh light and saw that there were four men in the vault room—Harris, Sayers, and two others she had never seen before. Sayers and Harris both had guns leveled at her.

"I don't believe it," she said, trying to pull it off as a huge joke.

"You did an excellent job getting in here," Harris said. "My foreign visitors here were quite impressed with your abilities. They're most anxious to . . . to take you apart and study you."

It wasn't a joke. Jaime felt her body go limp in terror. But her bionic legs didn't go along with her natural human weakness. She stood her ground and tried not to look as scared as she felt.

"I do caution you not to make any foolish moves," Harris said. "You are swift, but you can't outrun a bullet. And my friends here can study you dead as well as alive. Now, then, if you'll come along quietly . . ."

He waved his gun for her to turn around, but his expression changed as he looked past her toward the door of the vault. She whirled around to see Donald standing there. He, too, held a gun, but it was pointed at his father.

"No," Donald said. His mouth was drawn in a tight line, and he had clearly, finally, made his decision.

"Donald..." Harris sounded more annoyed than frightened.

"I won't let you do this," Donald interrupted his father.

"Don't be ridiculous. Put that gun down before you hurt someone."

"Don't tell me what to do, Dad. Not any more. Come on out, Jaime."

But Sayers was quick. He brought his own gun up quickly, knocking Donald's pistol from his hand.

Jaime kicked out with her foot, knocking Sayers against one of the foreigners with a powerful thrust that sent them both sprawling. In the same instant, she reached up with her right hand and ripped out the electric junction box from the ceiling. There was an explosion of live sparks and then total darkness inside the vault.

Jaime didn't slow down. She shoved Donald out of the vault door and followed him at bionic speed, slamming the heavy door closed right in the face of Carlton Harris. She would remember for a long time that last glimpse of his outrage. She turned to bend one of the locking bars on the vault and sealed it shut. She leaned against the door and waited for her breath to catch up.

The vault door was so heavy and so soundproof that even Jaime's right ear could pick up no sounds from inside, although she felt fairly certain there must be some heavy carrying-on in there. She looked over at Donald, who was slowly picking himself up from where she had thrown him.

"You okay?" she asked.

He stood up shakily. He nodded.

She looked at him sadly. "You know that I've got to call the OSI," she said.

He nodded again.

"Donald, I'm really sorry for you. Sorry that he's your father."

After a moment, Donald answered, "So am I."

Jaime reached out to touch his face. He raised his eyes to meet hers. Then he took her hand.

They left the building and the plant together. Jaime called Oscar from a pay phone on the corner, while Donald waited in the limousine to drive her home to Ojai.

Chapter Twenty

"...and we've finally got Carlton Harris right where we want him," Oscar said. "This is good coffee."

"Have another cup," Jaime said. "What about Donald?"

"He told me he was going to take a little time to collect his thoughts, and then look for a job with a law firm. He won't have any trouble. He did very well in college."

"That makes me feel a little better," Jaime said. She poured Oscar another cup of coffee, and he reached out to put a fatherly arm around her.

"You know, I'm really proud of you, Jaime. Steve will be, too."

"How is Steve?"

"Fine. He's finishing up in Thailand. He asked about you."

"Give him my love," she said. She picked up her books from the table. "Hey, do you realize that this is the first time you've sent me on a mission and I haven't